"You have t...
yourself."

Nikki flicked him a glance full of fear. "A child was stolen from his mother in Paris. I came to Zabbaran to find him."

Shakir shook his head. "I said the truth. Start again."

"It's the absolute truth."

"What would possess you to believe you have the knowledge or the strength to attempt such a daring feat?"

He hadn't realized how much he had begun to respect her unfamiliar and yet much stronger attitude. The new version of Nikki fascinated him.

"You give me all the information about the child," he began in his most convincing tone. "And then let me take you across the border tonight."

"I can't. I'm sorry, but I won't leave Zabbaran without him."

At this point she had nothing to lose by telling him the truth—at least part of the truth. "He's my child."

***

Become a fan of Silhouette Romantic Suspense books on Facebook.

Dear Reader,

Back we go to the fantasy world of the Desert Sons with the story of the middle son of the Kadir family, Shakir, perhaps my personal favorite of the three boys. He's a man strong of both body and will. He can tear a man apart with his bare hands and tear out your heart with his tender touch. Sigh.

In *The Sheik's Lost Princess,* we find the Kadirs involved ever more deeply in the covert war with their ancient enemies, the Taj Zabbar. While obtaining proof of terrorism to give to the authorities, the Kadirs have learned that Shakir's long-lost love, Princess Nicole, is being held in the desert kingdom controlled by the Taj Zabbar. Shakir has no decision to make. He will go to her rescue.

Have you ever wondered about a lost love? About what happened to them over the years? Well, *The Sheik's Lost Princess* takes those questions to brand-new heights. I loved writing it.

I hope you will enjoy finding out what happened to Shakir and Nikki while they were apart—and more important, what will happen once they are back together.

Happy reading,

Linda

LINDA CONRAD

The Sheik's Lost Princess

ROMANTIC

SUSPENSE

 SILHOUETTE BOOKS

ISBN-13: 978-0-373-27711-7

Recycling programs
for this product may
not exist in your area.

THE SHEIK'S LOST PRINCESS

Books by Linda Conrad

LINDA CONRAD

When asked about her favorite things, Linda Conrad lists a longtime love affair with her husband, her sweetheart of a dog named KiKi and a sunny afternoon with nothing to do but read a good book. Inspired by generations of storytellers in her family and pleased to have many happy readers' comments, Linda continues creating her own sensuous and suspenseful stories about compelling characters finding love.

A bestselling author of more than twenty-five books, Linda has received numerous industry awards, among them the National Reader's Choice Award, the Maggie, the Write Touch Readers' Award and the *RT Book Reviews* Reviewers' Choice Award. To contact Linda, read more about her books or to sign up for her newsletter and/or contests, go to her Web site at www.LindaConrad.com.

To a great group of bloggers: Jan Vautard, JanieC,
Ellen, Kelley Hartsell, Jessiecue, Elaine
and Tammy Y at the eHarlequin.com blog.
Thanks for the help. You guys rock!

Chapter 1

Shakir Kadir was living in a romance novel.

But no author would write such a fanciful plot. A beautiful princess kidnapped by an evil sultan and held captive in a harem? A daring rescue attempt by an ex-lover, parachuting in on a moonless night? Not many novels could be this outrageous. Yet here he was, stuck inside an unbelievable reality.

Would he end up the hero or the fool in this melodrama? It didn't much matter. Shakir could do no less for the woman he'd once loved—despite both his brothers' concerns to the contrary.

As he grimly waited for the chopper pilot to arrive at the jump zone coordinates, Shakir watched the desert floor below. Flying at low altitude through eerie darkness, the quiet drone of the Merlin Mk3's engine made talking difficult. But infrared night vision goggles allowed him to pick out objects despite the lack of light. He hadn't traveled to this desolate wasteland since he'd been a teen. But the backward country of Zabbarán had not changed all that much in the intervening years.

Without the aid of running lights, their chopper blew like smoke through starlit skies. Shakir recognized rock outcroppings and herds of sheep below them. He remembered that late at night the desert could be as lonely and as silent as death.

Attempting to focus his attention away from the coming mission, he thought of how he had come this far. His extended family had opted to form a new intelligence unit under his younger brother, Tarik's, control. Tarik, a genius in covert strategy, resigned his commission in the United States Special Forces in order to organize an undercover operation for the Kadirs. It was Tarik's embedded undercover operatives that had provided them with current maps and architectural drawings for a hostage rescue mission.

Shakir's new position was as head of black ops for the family. It still amazed him that the Kadirs had suddenly needed to organize and operate like an army during a time of war. The answer to why was complicated.

The Kadirs had been forced into engaging in a cold war of sorts with an old enemy, the Taj Zabbar clan. The Taj had initiated this conflict unilaterally a few months back, supposedly in revenge for centuries-old perceived grievances.

To Shakir's mind, that was just so much rhetoric and showed insane thinking.

The Kadir family were Bedouin peoples. Nomads. They did not claim any country as their own and had never occupied any territory with borders to defend. In the modern era, the Kadir family no longer belonged strictly to the desert. The family ran international shipping operations and traded legitimate goods between various countries of the world. So why should a nonviolent family of traders and shippers like the Kadirs be forced to engage in a fight with an ancient tribe of thieves and murderers? It didn't make sense.

The Taj Zabbar clan had recently won their independence from Kasht, a neighboring country. With their independence, the Taj gained control of the territory of Zabbarán, a vast desert with millions of barrels of oil lying directly beneath the surface of the land.

The Taj Zabbar's sudden great wealth seemed to have opened up painful memories and long-ago hurts for them, and now, apparently, they intended to get even for ancient grievances by destroying the Kadirs. It was not the peoples of Kasht, who had been their true oppressors, that the Taj wanted to hurt. No. The country of Kasht had licked its wounds and made trading pacts with the Taj. Then the imprudent Taj turned all their hatred to the task of injuring and destroying the Kadir family.

Shakir wasn't particularly politically-minded, but he would be willing to wager that money and power lay at the bottom of the Taj's cold war. Someday, he was sure the answers would come out. In the meantime, the Kadirs were fighting back and trying to reveal the truth of the Taj's intentions to the world.

"Brother." Tarik's whispered voice broke through the silence of his earpiece. "One last chance to back off this fool's errand."

"The hostage extraction is on," Shakir muttered through his lip microphone.

Tarik was convinced this journey would lead them into a trap. But then, Tarik's job entailed questioning everything, every fact and every rumor, until all answers became clear. Shakir's job, on the other hand, was black ops. See a problem. Fix the problem. By stealth or by force, whichever worked best.

The hostage rescue mission clearly seemed to require both. A group of western women were being held inside one of the Taj Zabbar's desert fortresses. The females had been either kidnapped or lured there to be auctioned off to the highest bidders. Great fortunes could be had by selling to the international pornography, sex and slavery trades.

The Taj Zabbar were well known as middlemen in every sort of illegal trade. It mattered little to them why their clients wanted the women. Only that they would pay dearly for them.

Shakir would never forget the exact moment he'd spotted the name *Nicole Olivier* on the list of abducted women that a Kadir undercover operative provided. Shakir had carried a mental picture of her around in his head for the past six years. But when he'd first read the name, he couldn't bring her face to mind. Years of trying to block her memory, and the hurt that went along with it, had temporarily wiped his mind clean.

But it didn't take long for everything to come back in a painful rush.

It was about that same time when his brothers had cautioned about any rescue attempt becoming a trap. Darin and Tarik both believed it was possible that the Taj Zabbar could've somehow learned of Shakir's old relationship to Nicole, the Princess of Olianberg. If that were true, his brothers worried that the enemy would be trying to lure the Kadir's middle son, Shakir, to Zabbarán for blackmail, or possible execution.

Shakir didn't buy it for a moment. Princess Nicole's family had been out of the news for several years. Ever since they were forced to abdicate their claims to the throne of their tiny European principality. After their failed coup attempt, the family had quietly dropped out of sight. Even Shakir could find no word of them.

When he'd first fallen for Nicole at university, the Olianberg royal family had insisted on keeping their only daughter's relationship to a Bedouin from leaking to the press. Shakir hadn't even realized it was a problem at the time because when they'd first met, Nicole had kept her royal heritage hidden from him, as well as from the rest of the world.

Coming back to the present, Shakir had no idea how the Taj had managed to capture Nicole. But he knew why. She was beautiful. Stunning. He was convinced the Kadir name had not come up in connection to hers. After their youthful affair had ended, the royal family seemed intent on burying the relationship, hopeful that no one would ever find out.

Giving his pack, chute and assault weapon one last check, Shakir turned the thumbs-up sign to his baby brother and the six other men on his team. Their plan was simple. They would drop into the country covertly, sneak into the fortress and rescue the women without drawing the attention of the main unit of fortress guards.

The operation had to be timed to the minute. Two hours and thirty-six minutes to be exact. Then they must return to the pickup point to meet the extraction choppers. In and out. Simple. He'd bloody well been through tougher assignments and hostage rescues during his years in a Royal Parachute Regiment in Afghanistan.

This one was a piece of cake.

Not long after they'd dropped into the desert, Shakir and Tarik stood in shadows at the base of a wall, waiting for the signal. Tall stone walls surrounded the enormous Taj fortress, but Kadir operatives had uncovered a secret passage to the inside.

The midnight chill crept into Shakir's bones as he waited and concentrated on executing his job. He shook it off, reminding himself not to let his mind slip. If he was to remain focused, he couldn't think about the possibilities—what he might find were the physical conditions of the women being held inside these walls.

The Taj Zabbar weren't noted for their humane treatment of prisoners. That these prisoners were also female did not bode well for their safety. So far the Kadirs hadn't found any tangible proof that the Taj Zabbar clan posed a threat to the whole world. But the Taj record on torture and abuse of their own citizens and neighbors, including women and children, was legendary.

Two clicks sounded in his earpiece.

"There's the signal," Tarik whispered. His brother disappeared into a nearly invisible slit in the wall and three of the men fell in behind.

Shakir hefted his Israeli-made Micro Tavor assault rifle, adjusted his NVGs and moved out, protecting their six. By using a grappling hook, the Kadir rescue unit hoisted each other over the outer perimeter walls and down onto the first in a series of multi-level lawns, porches and terraces.

Instead of making their way straight to the main house, the little troop of rescuers turned south and crouch-walked along the inner wall, heading toward a smaller building with Moorish influences. The small house, originally used as a Kasht palace, was now used as the harem for the new Taj fortress that had been built around it.

The main quarters of the new fortress, recently constructed by a Taj Zabbar elder, were reputed to be a showplace. With ornate tiled halls, splashy and expensive artwork and lavish furnishings, the palace was ripe with ostentatious wealth and fit for the elder Umar. He had spared no expense to make it a true paradise on earth.

Shakir didn't need to see the new palace to dislike everything about it. His mission was clear. Following the others, he made his way down the wall to the small ancient building situated to the east of the main palace.

When the Kadir troop quietly entered the former concubines' quarters, Shakir noticed immediately that the Taj elder had done nothing to modernize these original buildings. Faded oriental carpets covered the floors, exactly as they had done for a hundred years. Cracked and stained rock walls and winding, narrow hallways led them through a maze of tiny, dark rooms.

It was a good thing he was wearing NVGs. But it was by using only his more feral abilities, the ones honed and trained by his warrior grandfather, that Shakir recognized the distant scent of precious water.

Intel claimed the women were being held in a private chamber beside the ancient harem baths. He caught the slight whiff of mold, heard the low drip of water and led the way.

As the unit of Kadir men silently crept forward toward the baths, Shakir's mind went back to the first time he had ever seen Nicole. It seemed like a lifetime ago. He'd been a lonely outcast, barely surviving his first year at a British university. She was the shy but beautiful student from some unheard-of European country who had offered to tutor him in English.

They'd struck up the friendship of two misfits. Then slowly the friendship developed into a romance. He'd fallen hard. But when she'd finally confessed the truth of her royal background and told him she was promised to a man that she'd never met, he walked away without a fuss.

Only to die a thousand solitary deaths in the six years since.

Scrubbing the back of his hand across his eyes to wipe away the sweat, Shakir checked those memories. No point in a rehash. The past was in the past. Today, the mission was rescue—not reopening a festering sore that would never heal.

Another click sounded in his earpiece, and he halted mid-stride. They'd come to the door leading to the women's damp prison. Tarik and one other man peeled off from the group to dispatch the two guards—unseen, but nevertheless standing between their position and the chamber.

Counting down, Shakir gave his brother thirty seconds and then led the way into the harem with his weapon at the ready. It was a huge open room, with gigantic columns rising thirty feet or more and then disappearing into the darkness of a vast ceiling. Low torch lights reflected off the rippling waters of the bath.

He pushed the NVGs up his forehead and searched the shadowed chaise longues and steps beside the pool, looking for Nicole. Two of the women he'd also expected to find slept fitfully on top of ratty-looking beds. Two others reclined on the steps, staring bug-eyed off into a nonexistent distance. The whole atmosphere reminded him of an opium den he'd once visited in his rougher days.

"They've been drugged." Tarik came up behind him, whispering low. "We expected something like this. But it will make it tough leading them to freedom in their condition."

Tarik spun in a circle and counted heads. "Have you spotted her yet?"

"She isn't here." Shakir didn't know whether to be relieved or panicked.

He went with *standby* mode. "Take these four and move out. I'll keep looking."

Tarik nodded and silently crept away toward the closest woman. Shakir was grateful that his brother had not mentioned the obvious. Time would not allow an extensive search. If he didn't locate Nicole soon, the extraction choppers would leave without them.

As he flipped the NVGs back over his eyes and moved into darkness, Shakir's lifetime of training overruled his all-too-human mind. Long ago he had developed the instincts of a predator. A hunter. He would use those instincts now to locate his former lover.

And he would not allow himself to dwell on the

other possibilities. He would not consider the chance that Nicole may have already been sold into slavery. Or that the Taj elder might have picked her out for his own household. Or that she had already been accidently given a lethal overdose of the drugs.

Shutting out any of those potential pitfalls, he moved swiftly. Those thoughts were inconceivable and therefore they did not exist.

Not for the hunter.

"Your plan is too dangerous, miss. Please reconsider." The old handmaiden's shoulders were rounded and bent and her ancient eyes watery. But her sharp gaze seemed bright with intelligence, good sense and a healthy dose of fear.

Nikki Olivier went against her better judgment and hugged the woman. "I must go tonight, Lalla. I cannot manage another day of pretending to take the drugs. The guards will soon uncover my stash of unused pills and you and I will both suffer the consequences."

"But if given another day or two..." The old woman continued with her pleading. "The moonlight will guide your way to the coastal village of Sadutān. The Zabbarán desert is full of dangers on moonless nights, but you dare not travel during the day."

The old woman named Lalla had done so much for her. Grateful, Nikki wanted to ask about her nationality in order to carry a message back to her family. Nikki had grown curious about where the old woman had originally come from before she'd been bound into slavery. Her accent sounded eastern European, but Lalla spoke both French and English fairly well, along with a generous knowledge of the language of her captors. How long had this poor soul been a household slave for the Taj elder?

Nikki decided to keep her questions to herself. She did not wish to share her own secrets and asking curious questions could only bring trouble.

"I have a broad knowledge of astronomy, Lalla. I shall have little difficulty navigating by the stars."

Lalla opened her mouth, then shut it again without any more words of caution. "Here is the boot polish, miss. Your nose requires another coat."

Nikki rubbed the foul stuff over the bridge of her nose. The boot polish mixed with soot that she'd used as a disguise had turned her skin a warm brown. She wiped her hands, pulled her precious map from the folds of her robes and moved closer to the nearest light source, wanting to study her route.

Going to Sadutān was not her plan. But she didn't want anyone, not even Lalla, to know her true destination. If, after she was gone, the Taj elder tortured Lalla for information, the old woman would be unable to tell him anything useful.

What a dismal thought. Nikki couldn't help feeling guilty and tried once again to plead her case. "Please come with me, Lalla. I beg you. Do not stay behind."

Lalla dropped her gaze to the floor in an imitation of the way Taj women behaved. "It is too late for me. Too many years have passed. If God wishes to bring me home, I am ready to go."

The old woman was talking about dying. Suicide by torture. Nikki felt fresh tears threatening to ruin her makeup job but she held them back. She had to stay strong.

"You are young and you have a mission yet to accomplish," Lalla added more forcefully than Nikki would've thought possible. "A mission best undertaken alone. Someone waits for you to change destiny. You must succeed in those efforts."

Now how could she know that? How could this old woman possibly know that Nikki had voluntarily come to Zabbarán to search for her son? She had told no one.

Thinking back on the whole sordid story of arriving in Zabbarán expecting to find a new job waiting for her as promised, only to be thrust into a dank cave-like prison with five other women, was not something Nikki did often. She didn't know what the Taj elder had in mind for her future now but knew it wouldn't include a legitimate job.

She'd come to Zabbarán with high hopes of locating her baby, and she would find him, or die in the attempt.

Truthfully, Nikki's first unforgiveable mistake had been in trusting her Parisian neighbor to watch her little boy while she went to work. That mistake had been the start of this journey through hell.

But, in her own defense, she'd been desperately poor at the time and her child had needed food and a place to live. After her father died, Nikki was left with no choice but to go to work. And there had been no friends or family to babysit her son while she worked.

Still, in retrospect, that seemed like a lame excuse. But at the time she was trying to be a good parent. The neighbor woman had actually seemed rather sweet and was good with children. She was kind. And, she already watched over other children from their building.

Nikki had checked around for another job, desperate

to find a different solution. Eventually, she'd given in and handed over her five-year-old boy for eight hours a day to a woman she barely knew.

Then the day arrived when Nikki came home to find her son, the neighbor and all the neighbor's possessions gone. It was her worst day—in a lifetime filled with bad days.

Nikki flew straight to the Paris police who looked at her as if she had sprouted wings. "Sorry, madame. We will take the report. But many children disappear each year in Paris. Not many are ever found. We will do our best."

Fighting hysteria and with no one to help her, Nikki beat on every door in her apartment building, searching for anyone with information. Her tears did not open any mouths, but eventually she sank to threatening people with bodily harm. That bought her a little information.

She was told the neighbor who'd disappeared with her baby had bragged about selling two of her charges to a desperate middle-eastern couple. The couple supposedly had wanted sons and were willing to pay a fortune to obtain them. Greed. Her son was taken from her because of greed. The more she thought of it, the more it made her sick to her stomach.

Nikki also learned that the middle-eastern couple claimed to be from a small town in the newly freed country of Zabbarán. She rushed back to the police with the news. They took the information and shrugged. Then they suggested she hire a private detective.

Too low on funds to consider such a solution and now frantic with worry, Nikki badgered everyone she met for ideas on how to get her son back. Eventually she was introduced to a man, who knew of a man, who was recruiting westerners for jobs in the new country of Zabbarán. She'd jumped at the prospect.

The next thing she knew, she'd landed in this horrible place. If it hadn't been for Lalla…

"You must adjust the moustache, miss."

Nikki refolded her map and put it away before pressing down against the smattering of dark hair she'd glued to her upper lip. "How is the disguise?"

"You will not fool anyone for long. Your feminine figure stands out even under the manly robes. Try to avoid encounters. And…" Lalla reached under her own robes and withdrew a dagger. "If you are attacked, use this wisely."

Staring down at a wide blade attached to a short leather hilt, Nikki tried to imagine using such a blade on a human. It was unthinkable—until she considered her son. For his sake, she would use any weapon at her disposal.

Reaching out to take the knife, Nikki froze with her arms stretched wide. One second ago she and the handmaiden had been alone in the harem's kitchen. The next instant she'd felt another presence behind her back, joining them in the room. Her instincts went on alert.

But before that fact had time to sink in, Nikki was attacked and roughly thrown to the floor. The dagger flew from her hands and clattered against the stone as the fall took her breath. Sucking in air, she fought to move. But as she tried to squirm out of the way, she was pinned underneath the hard planes of a man's body.

A big man.

Chapter 2

Shakir silently pointed the older woman into a corner, jammed the barrel of his weapon to the base of the young Taj soldier's skull and ordered the kid to be silent. The soldier kept squirming and moaning. Pressing his advantage with a knee to the kid's kidney, Shakir tried to quiet the tango. He growled orders in both the Taj Zabbar language and in the few words of Kasht that he could remember.

"You are making a mistake," the old woman said in French.

He glared at her, flipped the tango to his back and began a rough pat-down. Sweeping his hands across the kid's shoulders and down his sides and legs, Shakir checked for more weapons. The sight of that ancient dagger had put him on alert. This young Taj soldier could be as deadly to the mission as a scorpion's sting.

Temporarily stashing his compact MTAR 21 in the pack on his back, Shakir used both hands to search. With his right, he checked between the kid's legs. While with his left hand, he rolled down under the soldier's armpits and around the rib cage.

"Bloody hell." Shocked, Shakir stepped back and stared down into surprised hazel eyes. "Blast it, who the devil are you?"

"I...I..." The female under his hands was at a loss for words. So was he.

Then it hit him—a few minutes too late. "Nicole?" He reached out to take her by the arm and pulled her to her feet.

"Shakir? Shakir Kadir? Oh, my God, what are you doing here? You scared me to death."

He took a step back and studied the form of the young man standing in front of him. Only now that he knew the truth, the form no longer even vaguely resembled a young man. He should've known.

But Nicole's honey-blond hair had been entirely tucked up under a purple-checked kuffiyah. Her skin beneath the Taj soldier's garments looked the color of splotchy brown dates. Her tiny feet—the feet should've been a dead giveaway—were encased in the smooth leather sandals prevalent in these desert regions.

"What is that ridiculous-looking thing you've stuck to your lip?"

She reached up, smoothing her finger along what looked like a line of dirt. "Just a bit of Lalla's hair. Doesn't it look like a moustache?"

"Not even a little."

She grimaced, but immediately recovered her composure. "I don't understand. This is crazy. Like a bad dream. What are you doing here, Shakir?"

His initial flood of relief at finding her alive gave way to irritation and he, too, grimaced. "We've come to bring you home." She didn't look injured, but what had they done to her mind?

Where was her gratitude? Where were the tears of joy he had expected to see?

Antsy and ready to move out, Shakir fought his annoyance and reached for her arm. "Let's go."

Nicole jerked back. "Where?" She fisted her hands on her hips and glared at him. "How did you find me? Why are you really here?"

Stunned, Shakir saw the mistrust in her eyes and it wounded his pride. Never in their entire relationship had he given her reason not to trust him.

And he didn't have time to deal with it here. "We'll hash this out later. The choppers won't wait."

She stood her ground. Something odd was going on behind those eyes. Something very odd.

"*Now,* Nicole." He started toward her again.

"I was about to leave on my own." She backed up a step. "What about the other women?"

"I brought in a team. They're rescuing the other women at this moment. Everyone will leave the country in choppers as a group. *Everyone.*" His whole body hummed with impatience. "Do I have to carry you?"

"What about Lalla? We can't leave her behind."

For the first time, Shakir turned his head to study the old woman in the corner. Speaking to her in French, he asked, "Are you willing to leave?"

"I cannot. I have family who…I cannot, sir."

The old woman was not Taj. That much was clear. But

how long had she been living with them? Long enough to bear Taj children?

Suddenly, the old woman was too much of a liability to leave behind—but killing her was out of the question. "Sorry. You go with us."

Moving with the speed of lightning, Shakir grabbed the old woman up with one arm, then swung around and picked up Nicole with the other. Neither of the women was a burden. Both weighed less than his backpack. The old woman went limp against his side, but Nicole was another matter.

She didn't shriek or call out but beat at him with her fists. "Put me down. I can walk."

He hesitated. "Will you behave? If I set you down, you must keep up. And you must do exactly as I say. Everything. Understood?"

Nicole nodded but kept her mouth closed. Good girl.

He lowered her to her feet. "We don't have a lot of time left."

Taking her elbow, he guided her out into the narrow hallway. Once again in darkness, he flipped the NVGs over his eyes. But he didn't really need infrareds to see. He had memorized every inch of the maze inside this building and they weren't that far from an exit. He could make it blindfolded.

Moving like a cat, Shakir let his instincts take control. He wanted to blank his mind, to act as he had been trained—without thought. But that look in Nicole's eyes still bothered him.

He tried to reconcile the tough woman in a makeshift disguise with the sophisticated royal he had once both loved and then hated, but couldn't make the connection.

In a way, he should be impressed with her. Impressed that she would've taken the initiative to disguise herself and try to escape on her own. The Nicole he remembered was a follower, not a leader.

Slanting her a glance in the dark, he wondered what kind of person this new Nicole had become. And if he would care for her as much as the Nicole he'd fallen in love with long ago. So far, that seemed highly unlikely.

Nikki let Shakir lead them out of the harem and into the fresh air. She still couldn't believe it was really him. When he'd first said her name, shock waves of memory blasted right through her system like an earthquake.

Of all the people in the world. Why now?

There'd been a time when she would have given ten years of her life just to see him again. To hear him say her name. To have him tell her what to do.

But that was long ago. A different lifetime.

In this lifetime, he presented a threat. Oh, not that she thought he might hurt her. She knew without question that he would never do such a thing.

No, the biggest threat Shakir posed today was that he had a different agenda from hers. Nikki wasn't sure exactly what his agenda entailed. But she knew he must have some reason for showing up here in Zabbarán all of a sudden. Since he couldn't possibly know what she needed most, what she longed to get back, he could not be trusted.

It didn't take much for her mind to travel from that thought to the next—she might not trust him, but she could use him. She'd seen the light in his eyes when he'd first realized it was her under the makeup. She'd also caught his slight distraction whenever they touched. He'd felt that instant charge the same way as she had. He still had feelings for her.

But Nikki could not let her own distraction deter her from her goal. She would use the charge between them, that sexual awareness, to her best advantage.

With Lalla thrown over his shoulder, Shakir led Nikki through the gardens toward the outer perimeter wall. He was heading toward the hidden gate. She'd been told by Lalla that no one else knew about the almost invisible exit in the wall.

Squaring her shoulders, Nikki prepared for a surprise confrontation at the gate. If he knew about it, others might know and be waiting. This could be some kind of trap. Nikki only wished she still had the dagger that Shakir forced her to leave behind.

When they reached the farthest wall, Shakir leaned down and whispered, "We're late. Make no noise."

Noise was the last thing she had on her mind when freedom was this close. She froze, silent and panting, as he released her to lean against the wall.

The gate was nearby. Only a few yards away, but Shakir didn't move in that direction. Instead, he ignored the gate and withdrew a long doubled up rope with a hook arrangement on the end and began twisting it in his hands. In a few seconds, he pitched the hook end up and over the ten-foot wall. A distant clank told her the hook had hit something solid on the other side.

After another few rope maneuvers, Shakir turned to her. "You first. Put your foot in the loop. I'll hoist you to the top of the wall. Wait for us there."

One second's hesitation was all she allowed herself. She slid her sandal into the loop, locked her knee and hung on to the rope with both hands. The ride to the top went quickly and she crawled up on the wide ledge. Taking a breath, she dropped the rope loop back over the same way she'd come up.

Nikki couldn't imagine how Shakir would be able to climb up on his own, especially since he had to carry Lalla. But moments later he was standing beside her.

"Down is trickier," he whispered. "Got the nerve to try it? Or shall I make two trips—one for you and one for the old woman?"

"Tell me what to do."

Shakir gave her a quick lesson in rappelling. If Nikki hadn't been so scared, she might have hesitated to go backward over the edge. But she was determined not to draw any attention or cause any trouble.

Not until the last second when she could make a break for it. Shakir and the others might be leaving by helicopter, but she wasn't leaving Zabbarán. Not without her son.

She still had her map, her compass and the ability to navigate by the stars. And she could rely on her wits. The only difference now was that with all the others leaving by helicopter, her captors would assume she had left the country as well. They would not be quite as quick to give chase.

Her goal remained the same. She had come to this country to rescue her son.

Dragging Nicole by her arm and carrying the old woman, Shakir traipsed across the sands to a stand of date palms not twenty yards away from the wall. He used a simulated high-pitched falcon whistle to warn the others of their approach.

Out of the darkness, Tarik appeared like a ghostly spirit and handed him a canteen. "The others have already headed for the coordinates. The women hostages are so drugged, they've been no trouble. There's not much time left and ten miles to travel."

Shakir took the first sip then put the canteen to the old woman's lips and waited for her to drink. She was not cooperative but he forced her to swallow a couple of priceless drops. Afterward, he handed the canteen over to Nicole.

"I'll take the old woman," Tarik told him. "You take Nicole. We can make better time if we carry the women rather than try to walk them that far."

Shakir nodded at his brother and turned to Nicole. "This may not be comfortable, but it's for the best."

"Stop…"

Not waiting for her to complain uselessly and waste any of their precious time, he hoisted Nicole over his shoulders and moved out behind Tarik. It was a difficult ten miles over rough terrain to the extraction point and he knew she would never make it under her own power. This was the only way for them to arrive in time.

At any point along the way, if either of these two women cried out for some reason, all of them would be at the mercy of the Taj Zabbar soldiers. Sounds traveled far in the night desert air. Explaining that to Nicole now, however, was impossible. He had to hope against hope that she was smart enough to keep silent.

In his opinion, the going was easy but too slow. He tried to follow an old camel trail, but sand had blown over it in spots and drifts were several feet deep in many places.

Carrying Nicole wrapped around his neck and draped

on his shoulders was the easiest part. She was as light as a bird. He didn't remember her body being this lean in the past. Perhaps the Taj had starved her while she was their prisoner. That notion made him grit his teeth.

After they were flown to freedom and had a moment to reflect and talk, he wanted to ask her how she had come to be captured by the Taj. Had they taken her by force? Shakir didn't like the idea of that any better than the idea of her starving at their hands.

After her initial surprise at being carried, Nicole's body relaxed and she was completely silent during their march across the sand. Grateful for the favor, Shakir only wished he could've had a moment to still her fears and calm her down before they began the trip. Grabbing her up like a bag of sheep feed and slinging her over his shoulder seemed barbaric. Like something he may have seen done to women back when he'd learned to live as a desert warrior at his grandfather's knee.

The more he thought about it, the more horrified he was by his own savage reaction. Despite having done it for her best interests, he knew she would never forget. He could only hope she would be able to forgive him someday, though he doubted if he could forgive himself.

They ended up covering the ten miles of desert in good time. In a little over two hours, he looked ahead and spotted the chopper hovering over a wide flat surface. The other members of the team were boarding with their human cargo.

Worried that they were too exposed in the open desert, Shakir halted about fifty yards shy of the pickup zone and lowered Nicole to the ground beside a creosote bush. "Sit and stretch your legs out in front of you for a moment. I'm going in closer to help load the other women. For safety's sake, I'll board you at the last possible second. I don't want to take any chances on surprise sniper fire. Think you can walk?"

Rubbing at her feet to get the circulation back, Nicole looked up at him with that strange expression in her eyes again. "I can walk. May I have the canteen?"

His heart went out to her. Handing the water over, he thought back to the sophisticated but fragile princess who had once captured his heart. She was holding up quite well under the strain.

But they had no time to reminisce. Perhaps later. After he'd rescued her and explained how he'd known of her plight. It was a long story and their minutes left in Zabbarán were coming to an abrupt end.

"I'll signal when it's your turn to board. If you can't walk, I'll come back for you."

"I said I can walk."

She was trying hard to be strong. It made him yearn to take her in his arms and hold her close to his chest, encasing her in a protective embrace. Instead, he nodded sharply, turned and made a dash for the chopper.

Within a few minutes, Tarik loaded the old woman, the last of the hostages to board except for Nicole. Through his earpiece, Shakir heard one of the Kadir surveillance teams warning that a Taj Soviet-made Ilyushin IL-28 was scrambling from the country's main landing strip a couple of hundred miles away. The old-model jet was known to be a dilapidated bucket of bolts. But still, it would be here within minutes.

"Now or never, brother." Tarik turned and held out his hand.

Shakir swivelled, signalling to Nicole. The chopper's

rotors blew sand in wide circles around the landing zone. He was suddenly worried that she would not be able to see his signal and started running toward her position.

Calling her name, he closed the distance between the chopper and where he'd left her waiting. No answer.

"Sixty seconds," Tarik shouted through his earpiece.

Shakir arrived at the creosote bush, but the space was empty. No Nicole. He made a cursory inspection of the surroundings. No Nicole.

"Thirty seconds."

Bugger it. Bugger her.

"Go!" he shouted to his brother.

"Not without you." Tarik's voice was too sharp. His brother was worried about him.

"I'll be okay." Shakir worked to sound calm, confident. "I'm not leaving without her, Tarik. I'll contact you as soon as I can. Now, go!"

Nikki never imagined it would be this difficult to find her way across the desert by using the stars. Lalla had marked the coordinates of every water hole, oasis and town within a hundred-mile radius on her map. But now that Nikki was out here, it all looked the same in the pitch-black night.

Luckily, the house where her son was supposedly living was only about fifty miles from the fortress she'd left behind. She could certainly make a fifty-mile walk in a couple of long nights' worth of travel. It was true, though, that she would need fresh water and places to rest during daylight hours. In addition to being impossible to travel during the heat of the day, she needed to keep the Taj Zabbar soldiers from spotting her in the desert.

Stopping for a moment, she breathed deep and used one of her precious matches to check her map. That water hole should be right here. She needed to find it before daybreak.

Surely she wouldn't have the bad luck to get lost on her first night. Yes, she'd gotten a bit turned around while being carried on Shakir's shoulders. But she had been sure that she'd reoriented herself properly within the first few moments on her feet.

Still a bit curious about how he had known to come for her in the first place, Nikki felt guilty about her disappearing act. But Shakir hadn't allowed her any time to speak. And hers was a story that needed more than a cursory explanation.

After she found her son and rescued him, maybe then she would try again to locate Shakir. To talk. Of course, the last time she'd tried to find him things hadn't worked out well.

Thoughts of that dark time, those long months, surrounded her in a swirl of sadness. It had been the beginning of a whole new life. And she had drastically changed from those difficult days to today.

Nikki often wondered how different her life might have been had she found Shakir back then. But what-ifs and maybes were a part of her past now. She could no longer afford to dwell on how things might have been.

Turning in a complete circle, Nikki looked up at the stars once more. That watering hole had to be close.

"You're almost there." The male voice, coming out of the darkness, nearly caused her to turn tail and run.

"Shakir?" It had to be him. She had heard that voice

often enough in her dreams. "How in the world did you find me here?"

He was beside her in an instant. "We'll talk about it later. For now, we need to take shelter and stop standing out in the open."

Grabbing her elbow, he whirled her around. He didn't take more than fifteen steps before a rock outcropping appeared silhouetted in the darkness.

"Why didn't you fly off with the others?" She was confused and felt a growing annoyance at his showing up when she least expected it.

"I should also ask why you didn't get on the chopper." His pointed reply was not an answer. "But both our questions will have to wait. Trouble is coming. We need to hunker down."

"The Taj Zabbar soldiers? They found me?"

"No." Marching them straight past a stand of scrawny trees, Shakir leaned in close. "Hell is on the way."

"Hell?"

"Scourge of the desert, Nicole. *Sandstorm.*"

Chapter 3

*S*andstorm?

Nikki had heard of them, of course. But she never dreamed they could be a problem for her in Zabbarán.

"Could the storm kill us?"

"No." Shakir put his arm around her shoulders, guiding them closer to the boulders. "But we must take precautions."

Why hadn't she noticed anything wrong before he showed up? Was he lying to her about a sandstorm coming? For what reason?

She'd learned the hard way not to trust anyone. Never again would she allow herself to be taken in by a sincere-looking face and a kind manner.

As she let Shakir lead her toward a two-story mound of shale and rocks, Nikki paid closer attention to her surroundings. Yes, she could feel a slight increase in the wind's velocity, but at this point she was only aware of a nice quiet breeze on her face. Looking around, she also noticed the pale beginnings of lavender light and knew that in the desert that meant daybreak would soon appear in all its magnificence.

Things were never as scary in the light of day as they seemed in the dark.

After climbing up a medium grade to the base of giant rock boulders, Shakir pealed off his backpack. He crouched beside her on the stony ground and opened his pack.

While searching through the pockets, he made a demand. "Give me the canteen."

Feeling at a loss, she was in no position to argue. At least temporarily she had no choice but to let him make his demands. She gave him the canteen and he used the water to dampen a tan-colored cloth. Then he handed the cloth to her.

"What is this? Your wet T-shirt? What do I do with this?"

The predawn glow gave her enough light to see his eyes. Warm, liquid brown and fringed by long, ebony lashes, those fascinating eyes were a reminder of a time past. Whenever she'd gazed into them in her youth, she'd ended up swamped in a pool of longing and need. There was a time when she had trusted him implicitly to do the right thing. Not anymore.

"After we take cover," he shouted, "hold the shirt over your eyes, nose and mouth. Breathe through it and don't stop until I give the okay."

"Cover?" Turning in a circle, she looked around and saw nothing but rocks and sand dunes. "Where?"

Shakir didn't answer but stood and hurried over to a

nearby rock-covered stand. Even through the low light, she realized this must be the water well she had been expecting to find. While lifting the large flat rock from its base, his muscles rippled and bunched under his shirt. The sight gave her an unwelcome tingle, forcing her to dig her fingernails into her palms to stay quiet.

Once Shakir had the heavy-looking rock in his arms, he used it to cover the well. Every one of his movements was economical, as though he'd been taught exactly what to do.

After returning to her side, he said, "Let's go."

Huh? "I don't think…"

"Look." He pointed off in the opposite direction of the rising sun.

She turned her head and got one of the biggest shocks of her life. The entire horizon, from desert floor to electric-blue sky, was blurred by a clay-colored cloud. A towering line of menacing dust blocked out both sky and land as it rolled over the dunes. The storm appeared to be headed right for them.

Maybe some things *could* be scarier in the day-light.

Shakir scooped her up next to his side and ran toward a cleft in the rocks. As they came closer, she managed a better look at the indentation in the rocks. The space seemed tiny. But never hesitating for a second, he pushed her into the small crevice.

"Cover!" He jammed in close behind her, blocking her body with his own.

Nikki had enough room and time left to raise her hands and cover her face with the wet cloth. In the next instant, a deafening roar overtook them.

The sounds of angry sands, fiercely pounding against

solid stone, assaulted her eardrums. Winds roared in her ears even under the protective head scarf she still wore. Biting the inside of her cheek, she waited.

Those initial dire seconds of the storm soon turned to long desperate minutes of panic, and finally dragged on interminably for what seemed like hours. Between bouts of panic, boredom and spurts of claustrophobia, she had time to think. Time enough for the stillness of a memory.

A memory from long ago. One sunny summer day when the sky over the English countryside was not blurred with sand, but was so clear and blue it could bring one to tears. That afternoon had been meant for young lovers. It was one of those days meant to fool them into believing that true love would last forever.

But even then, as lost as she'd been in her dreams of lust and in an intense pair of chocolate eyes, in the back of her mind she must have known that love was not the road to happiness. Not for her.

Still, for those few precious months with Shakir, she had let herself believe in the dream.

She'd wanted desperately for Shakir to make things different for them. In her naïveté, he had been everything she'd thought she needed. Everything she had ever wanted. Tall, broad and so good-looking that other girls swooned over him, he was a dashing prince of the desert. An intelligent, modern-day sheik who would carry her off to a fantasy life in some faraway romantic land.

Unfortunately, it hadn't taken long for her to awaken from the dream. Her eyes had been opened when her parents began demanding that she come home and take up her royal life. The life she had been raised to obediently follow.

Nikki did her duty, stepped up and complied with her parents' bidding. She sent Shakir away. But secretly, as she had spoken those hateful words of goodbye, she'd hoped against hope that he would not leave willingly. She wanted him to take a stand and make his own demands.

Wishing for him to love her enough to fight for her, Nikki had held her breath. She waited for Shakir to plead his case and offer to steal off with her and hide from her responsibilities.

But he never did. Shakir never demanded anything. He simply hadn't loved her enough to fight. He'd heard her out, then turned silently and walked out of her life for good.

What had become of him since? she wondered. It was a question that had haunted her for many years. Perhaps once the storm was over, she would finally get the answers to her burning questions. But she would have to be smart when she asked those questions. Smarter than she had ever been in her past.

With disappointment after disappointment, she'd grown much wiser over the years. And she knew how to be careful. Particularly careful with what she said.

Shakir felt Nicole's legs giving way just as the last of the sandstorm's winds rolled off into the distance like the waning echo of a ringing bell. His own limbs were stiff from standing, but he eased back and let her limp body slide into his arms.

"We were lucky," he said as he lifted her and carried her out of their narrow rock shelter. "The storm was a small one."

Still holding the by-now dry T-shirt, her hands

dropped to her chest and she blinked her eyes against the bright sun. "You call that small?" Choking on her words, she tried to swallow past the build up of dust in her throat. "How long were we standing there?"

"A few hours." He understood how she felt. His throat was parched and gritty, too, and tiny grains of sand layered every bodily crevice.

He helped Nicole ease herself onto a nearby flat-surfaced rock. Then he pulled off his goggles and earpieces and looked around the small area surrounding the water hole.

Checking his watch, he discovered the sand had blasted the clear face and he could no longer make out the time. "Sandstorms can sometimes last for days."

"Days? I wouldn't have been able to stand for that long."

He would've seen to it that Nicole stood for however long the storm took. Even if the winds carried on for a week. He had sworn to let nothing happen to her. Nothing.

The sun shone from directly overhead, making Shakir give thanks to the desert mother that it was spring season and not the dead of summer. Still, during the hottest part of the day, extreme heat could rise to uncomfortable levels even in the spring months.

Within a minute or two of scouting the area, he found what he'd been seeking. A makeshift shelter from the sun formed underneath a natural rock ledge. As was the case at many desert water holes, long ago desert travelers had constructed a shelter to provide shade for daylight resting periods. Generations of travelers had used the shelter ever since.

Shakir hadn't bothered to look for the shelf to use

as their shelter from the sandstorm. More of a cave-like structure, the shelter was too low to the ground to provide enough protection from blowing sands. He had learned in his boyhood that standing on higher ground made far more sense as defense against the winds. But used as a cool place to rest until dusk, this shallow cave would do fine.

Hanging tenuously on to the rough surfaces of the rock she'd been using, Nicole rose to her feet. Her knees wobbled for a moment, but eventually she managed to stand.

Once she was on her feet, deep ragged coughs began racking her body. He scolded himself for neglecting to see to her needs. What kind of a proficient desert rescuer was he? He handed over the canteen and helped her take a few swallows.

"Keep the canteen with you and take small swallows periodically over the next few hours while we are at rest. Don't gulp the water. Your body cannot absorb it yet."

She nodded that she understood. Shakir noticed then that his dehydrated body had also begun rebelling against the growing heat of midday. Shoving aside the piles of new sand, he removed the rock covering from the water well. After reopening the well, he moved as quickly as possible, refilling a collapsible bladder from his pack with the precious liquid.

Now they needed shelter. "Come on. It's time." He reached out, ready to take her by the hand.

Staring up at him, her eyes took on that distrustful expression once again. "Time for what? How did you find me in the dark anyway?"

Shakir grew irritated with her questions. He was the one who knew how to survive the desert. Knew it far too well, in fact. But as long as they were to remain in Zabbarán, for her own safety, she needed to defer to his judgment and experience.

After taking a deep, calming breath, he finally remembered that Nicole was a fragile creature. High-strung and spoiled. The princess was probably experiencing a form of PTSD due to her capture and imprisonment. He'd learned all about the psychology of victims during his training in modern warfare for the British. It would serve him well to keep that training in mind and try to put aside his ancient warrior training at the hands of his mother's father.

Nicole was a woman with no experience at hard living. As a princess royal she was more accustomed to servants and satin sheets, and he needed to cut her some slack.

"I found you by using the infrared goggles," he explained. "Spotted your footsteps in the sand as you walked away from the chopper. You made no attempt to hide your trail. Within a half mile I knew where you must be heading. Water is too precious in this country. You would surely stop at the closest well."

He wanted to ask why she hadn't jumped at the chance to leave with the other women. But he had a gut feeling that she wasn't yet ready to talk.

"It's time to take shelter from the sun, Nicole. Over there." He pointed out the low, dark cave at the base of the rocks.

"Oh. But…What if there are snakes in that cave? And other poisonous creatures might be hiding inside there as well."

Shakir took her by the hand. He made a pass and

grabbed his pack off the ground, then dragged both pack and woman across the sand.

"If we encounter snakes," he ground out, swallowing his annoyance at being questioned, "we will eat them. Other poisonous creatures will simply have to make room for us."

He felt a shudder ripple through her body and took small pleasure at giving her something else to think about. But as they crawled into the cool, shaded cave, he felt chagrined by his bad behaviour.

Years ago, as her lover and friend, he had never let his uncivilized side show. It had been easy to hide his true nature when he was around her during those halcyon days. She was soft and sweet and kind to a fault. Sophisticated and quiet, she'd been the antithesis of the life he had led up to that time.

Even as an inexperienced youth, he'd known their relationship was only a dream. That it could never last. And though he'd been shocked to learn she was a princess, he had not been surprised in the least when she told him goodbye. He'd expected that end to their affair from the beginning.

In a way, he'd even felt grateful to her for the reprieve. He had grown weary of trying to be someone he was not. His life with her had been in a kind of limbo up until then, living with the knowledge that at any moment a small slip in his behaviour would've shocked her into running away. He'd known it was only a matter of time.

Yes, he'd wanted her. But he had known from the start that an intelligent woman like Nicole would not stand for living with a man who couldn't control his baser instincts. At some point his true nature would've shown through. He couldn't have helped himself. It was a big part of who he was. A side of him built into his genetic structure.

For the entire time they'd been together, Shakir had lived on a razor's edge of self-control.

"It's cool in here," Nicole murmured after he found her a sandy spot to sit. She sounded surprised.

He wanted to take her by the shoulders and shake her—yell at her. As long as they were in the desert, she must learn that he knew best.

Instead, he merely nodded and asked, "Do you think you can eat something?"

"Not snake?"

He couldn't hold back the chuckle. "No, not snake. But you might like snake meat a lot better than you will one of these American-made MREs."

"MREs?"

"Armed services food. Meal, Ready-to-Eat. This one is meant to give you quick strength and stamina."

He handed the MRE over and showed her how to open the package. "This isn't much. But I didn't imagine we'd be trying to survive in the desert for this long."

Nikki would've liked to strangle Shakir with her bare hands for both teasing her about the snakes and for his wisecracks about surviving in the desert. But since he had knowledge of survival tactics that she didn't possess, she settled for strangling down the MRE.

"You appear extraordinarily hungry," he remarked as she concentrated on swallowing past her dry throat. "Most people in the desert lose their hunger to the heat. How long has it been since you've eaten anything?"

After struggling with the last bite of the MRE, she

said, "I haven't eaten since I came to Zabbarán. Maybe it's been a few days. I'm not sure."

"The Taj didn't feed you?"

She took a few more sips from the canteen. "The food they gave us was drugged. I did not dare to touch a bite."

"How'd you learn about the food being drugged?"

Nikki leaned back and closed her eyes, but her voice was rough. "Lalla took pity on me. We struck up a kind of friendship when I first arrived. She warned me not to eat, and she sneaked clean water in for me to drink."

"Don't think about it now. Rest."

With her eyes closed, Nikki's mind blocked out all the images of the past few days and she fell into a deep, dreamless sleep. When she awoke, she couldn't tell how much time had passed. But Shakir was still sitting in the same place and his eyes were still trained on her. Watching her closely.

"Feeling better? Sleeping should've helped."

She nodded and took a sip from the canteen.

"Nicole… What else did the Taj do to you while you were a captive?"

"Nothing much." She stretched and wiggled her toes. "They made all the women bathe and forced us to wear special robes. But Lalla told me the elder wanted to keep us pure for the auction. He wouldn't allow any of the guards to touch us."

Shakir grimaced and lowered his voice to a near whisper. "The Taj elder planned to auction off the women prisoners." He sounded angry. "Do you know to whom?"

She shrugged, but then she wasn't sure he was really

seeing her movements in the shade of their cave. He seemed lost in his own world.

"I think it was better that I didn't know. I've been having a hard enough time sleeping as it is."

Now why had she admitted that? It was a slip of the tongue she should not have made. And she had promised herself to be careful with her words.

Thankfully Shakir did not appear to catch her slip. She wasn't sure what she would've done had he asked her to explain her restlessness. Nikki would never rest again until her son was back in her arms.

Still staring out into dead space, Shakir nodded absently.

Finally he spoke. "How did the Taj capture you? Was it through violence? Were you injured?"

Uh-oh. This explanation could be a minefield if she wasn't extremely careful.

"No. I came here willingly. I thought I was coming to Zabbarán for a legitimate job. It wasn't until I arrived at their port city that I realized I was really a prisoner."

"A job?" Shakir sounded incredulous. "But why would someone like you, a royal princess, need to work?"

Damn it. She wasn't ready for this explanation yet. How could she be sure that he would not use her story against her somehow?

Who was he—really? He didn't seem like the same person she remembered loving in her college days. Who had he become over the years?

"Uh... Before I tell you *my* story, I need to hear yours. What are you doing here? What does your family, your wife, think of this? And tell me how you knew I was in Zabbarán and in need of help. You were looking for me when you came, weren't you?"

He took a couple of swigs from his water skin and then stared out at a spot over her shoulder. "That's a lot of questions." Then he pinned her with a sincere look. "I have no wife. No one who is waiting for my return. And as for why I was looking for you, my older brother, Darin, obtained a listing of foreign women being held prisoner in the Taj elder's fortress. I spotted your name on the list and knew I had no choice but to come for you."

"How did your brother get the list? Why would he even have access to such a thing?"

Sudden horrible ideas popped into her head and made Nikki tremble with nerves. Was Shakir's older brother supposed to have been one of the bidders? Had the Kadirs stolen the women out of the Taj prison so they wouldn't have to pay for them? Just who was she dealing with here?

She backed up as far into the cave as she could go.

"This may be hard for you to believe," Shakir began. "But the Taj Zabbar have declared a kind of cold war against the Kadir family."

"Why would they do that? And if they have, why hasn't it been on the news?"

His lips spread in a wry smile. "There was a time when you trusted everything I said." Sighing, he gave his head a slight shake. "I only wish I knew why they hate us today. Our old family legends say the two tribes have been enemies for over five hundred years. And supposedly about fifty years ago, my family took sides against the Taj Zabbar and sided with the country of Kasht, their neighbors.

"The Kasht government offered the Kadirs control of Zabbarán's only seaport. I guess my grandfather's generation decided that a deep water port was a good enough prize to trade arms to the Kasht. Unfortunately, those weapons allowed the Kasht to kill and imprison a hell of a lot of the Taj people—women and children included—before they could win their freedom a few years back."

"I can see why the Taj might hate you. But…"

He barked out a sharp laugh. "Yeah, I know. It was a long time ago, and revenge is an odd reason for war. Nevertheless, the Taj have already blown up one of our port facilities in America, killing a dozen people including my uncle. And we've tracked the Taj elders' movements as they've made several attempts to kill my brothers and me."

Shakir's unusual story rambled around in her head, while she tried to make sense of it. "I can't say I have any great love for the Taj Zabbar," she admitted.

But were the Kadirs any better? "I know firsthand that the Taj run their country like a medieval fiefdom. And they apparently have no trouble at all dealing with drug lords and mobsters from around the world. Still, if things are as bad as you say, I don't see why your family hasn't gone to the United Nations and the world community seeking help."

"How do you know we haven't?"

"I would've learned about it from the news."

He opened his hands, palms up, as if trying to find something he could say to make her understand. "The civilized world won't listen to us without proof. The Taj pretend to be weak and innocent. We've been forced to start up a covert defensive army of sorts, designed to gather as much information about the Taj and their activities as possible."

"So that's how you learned about the women prisoners being held for auction?" His explanation sounded logical enough.

She had no reason to doubt. She'd already found out just how sneaky and terrifying the Taj Zabbar could be.

"I didn't think the Kadir family had a home country." Could the Kadirs fight such a powerful enemy? "I mean, aren't you Bedouin? How can you possibly manage to protect yourselves without borders to defend?"

"It's not easy, Nicole. The Kadirs will have to become tougher than the Taj. Fortunately, some of us already are."

Chapter 4

"I see." The horrified expression on Nicole's face was no surprise, and Shakir didn't blame her in the least.

He'd deliberately neglected to tell her one thing. *This* Kadir son was already a tough, ruthless youth when they'd been involved in their college fling. He'd hid his true nature from her, from everyone, all along.

Perhaps it was best if she never learned the uncomfortable truth. Too much information could destroy lives as well as memories. And all he had to do to keep his secret was lead her out of Zabbarán to freedom tonight. Then they would never have to see each other again.

But, hell, he'd been trying to lead her out earlier, and they were within seconds of attaining that goal. She'd casually sneaked away from the chopper instead. Now he would have to find another way of taking her to safety. But somehow his brain wasn't processing those facts in the right way. Why hadn't she jumped at the chance to leave?

"All right, Nicole," he began, using his sternest tone. "I told you how I knew you were a prisoner in Zabbarán. It's your turn. I want to know why you didn't board the chopper for safety when rescue was offered."

"I didn't want to leave the country yet, obviously." She sniffed, looking down her nose at him. "And stop calling me Nicole. That's not my name anymore."

He was positive she had not married and ascended to the throne of her tiny country the way her parents had wanted. If she had, he would've heard the news long ago.

Her current snippy attitude put him at a loss. "Shall I address you as *Your Majesty?*"

She wrinkled up her nose and frowned.

"How about if I call you *Princess?* Would that suit you better?"

"I answer to the name Nikki now. Or sometimes to *Ms. Olivier*. The person you knew as Nicole has been gone a long time."

That reply brought up more questions than it answered. She hadn't said why and that made him curious. But Shakir decided against asking anything else. There was probably a long story behind both the name change and why she'd been seeking a job when she came here. He wasn't sure he wanted to hear any of it.

Their very survival meant he needed to extend his full focus toward getting them out of the country. Becoming caught up in her troubles was the last thing he could handle in the meantime.

He stole a glance at the lengthening shadows beyond

their cave's entrance. Daylight hours were growing short.

"Let's take this conversation outside while we test our leg muscles. Rest period is over."

Going up on all fours, he crawled out into the dry, fresh air. He wasn't sure what he would've done had she refused to follow. But fortunately, when he rose to his feet and turned around, she was right behind him. He took a sip of water and encouraged her to do the same.

Then he said, "Okay, I will ask once more and this time you'd better give me a straight answer. Why did you sneak away from the chopper? Why didn't you want to leave Zabbarán?"

Tracing a finger across her dry lips, she silently stared at him as if lost in thought.

"If you don't tell me, *Nikki,* I'll simply drag you across the desert tonight to the Zabbarán port city of Sadután. You know I can do it, too. The Kadir family has contacts there. If all else fails, I can either sail us out or fly us over the border in a stolen plane."

She made no reply.

"And I *will* do that with or without your consent if you don't start giving me answers." He narrowed his eyes and silently dared her to go against him.

"You can sail and fly both? I didn't know you were such a superhero."

He didn't crack a smile. "This isn't a joke. You have two seconds to explain yourself."

She looked away, while rubbing circles on her stiffened knee and elbow joints. "To start with, I didn't come to this horrible country for a job. That was only the excuse I used to earn the airfare. I came for…"

Her hesitation irked him. "Don't stop now. I need the truth."

She flicked him a glance full of fear. But he had not a clue what she might be afraid to say.

"Um… Look," she began hesitantly. "The truth is, a child was stolen from his mother in Paris. I came to Zabbarán to find him and take him home."

"What?" Her words made no sense. Shakir shook his head and put a hand on her shoulder. "I said the truth. Start again."

Ripping her shoulder from his light grip, she glared at him. "It's the absolute truth. A little boy…" Her breath hitched and she had to stop and breathe deeply for a moment. "Just a baby—really. Anyway, he was kidnapped and brought to Zabbarán. The Parisian police refused to do anything about it so I volunteered to bring him back."

"You?" The idea was almost laughable, but no one was smiling. Shakir put a hand to his aching temple.

"What would possess you to believe you have the knowledge or the strength to attempt such a daring feat?"

She fisted her hands onto her hips. "I made it this far, didn't I?"

Throwing his own hands in the air in frustration, Shakir turned in a wide circle, counting to ten under his breath.

Finally, he said, "This is crazy talk. No one in their right mind would trust you to carry out a rescue mission for their child. Why didn't the mother hire a professional to help if the police refused?"

"She didn't have any money and…" When he started to interrupt, Nikki waved him off. "And no friends or family, either. She had only me. I couldn't very well say no."

Her whole story was way beyond nuts. Shakir paced around the water well a few times, trying to process what she'd told him.

"All right, where is this supposed child being held?"

"This *quite real* little boy was brought to Zabbarán by a middle-aged couple who said they wanted the son they could never have. I was told…that is…the mother was told the couple lives in the small town of Kuh Friez."

"Kuh Friez? But that's nearly fifty miles away. It's high on the mountain slopes."

"Oh, well, I didn't know about the mountains. But fifty miles isn't so much."

Needing another moment, Shakir took a sip from his water skin and then proceeded to refill it at the well. When that chore was complete, he was somewhat calmer.

"Let's discuss this." He stretched out his hand to offer her a seat on the one flat-surfaced rock. She refused and folded her arms across her chest, glaring at him.

"All right then, *I'll* discuss it. In the first place, fifty miles in the desert while climbing rock-strewn mountain slopes could take you about ten nights' travel time. Even if you can find enough water during the trip, what do you propose to eat?"

She pursed her lips and narrowed her eyes but didn't open her mouth.

"In addition to that," he went on, "how do you plan on convincing the couple to give up the boy if you do finally arrive at Kuh Friez? If they're kidnappers, they could be dangerous. And thinking beyond that potential problem, how did you intend to get the child out of the country?"

Her shoulders slumped and she looked like he'd punched her in the gut. "I hadn't planned ahead that far. I didn't know Zabbarán and the Taj Zabbar were so...so..."

"Backward and dangerous?"

She nodded and covered her face with her hands. "I thought there would be police. Someone of authority who would help me."

He couldn't stand seeing her defeated. He hadn't realized how much he had begun to respect her unfamiliar and yet much stronger attitude. The new version of Nikki fascinated him.

"How about if we make a deal?"

She looked over at him with cautious hope in her eyes.

"You give me all the information about the child," he began in his most convincing tone. "And then let me take you across the border tonight. I promise that my brothers and I will come back for the boy after we've had a chance to make a decent rescue plan."

Hanging her head, she sat on the rock. "No." Her whispered answer was almost too quiet to hear. "I can't. I'm sorry, but I won't leave Zabbarán without him."

"You're being too noble!" The words exploded from his mouth. "There's such a thing as carrying a promise too far. Is there something you aren't saying? Is this mother blackmailing you? What has she got on you that you would go this far for someone else's child?"

Nikki jumped up, fighting her tears. Crying would get her nowhere.

At this point she had nothing to lose by telling him

the truth—at least part of the truth. "He's not someone else's child," she cried through muffled sobs. "He's my child. My baby. I must get him back. I must—or die in the attempt."

Shakir's mouth dropped open for a second. Soon enough, though, he recovered and stared at her suspiciously.

"You have a child? *Your son.*" His eyes widened in disbelief. "Why isn't the father here? Why would he let you take this much risk alone?"

Nikki nearly blurt out all of it, but she was still unsure of him. She had good reason to be wary.

"I'm a single, unwed mother, Shakir. I have no one to help me."

"Your parents?"

She shook her head. "My father died a couple of years ago. After his death, my mother developed a dreadful case of dementia. She's in a nursing home and barely remembers who she is anymore."

"Then tell me again why you couldn't hire a professional to take care of this for you."

"All the money is gone." She turned away in order not to face Shakir while she gave him the facts. "After my father lost his bid to retake the kingdom, he spent most of his remaining funds in vain attempts to overthrow his cousin. The small amount that was left after his death is going toward my mother's support."

"I…I…" Shakir's voice was rough, shaky. "Why didn't you marry that prince—your third cousin, wasn't it? What ever happened to your parents' arranged marriage plans?"

She swung back around to him, swiped at her eyes and tried a weak smile. "The deal fell through."

"I see." Shakir sat on the flat rock and drew his eyebrows down in thought.

He stayed quiet for a long time. Nikki kneaded her hands together over and over, wishing the two of them were still friends the way they had once been. But too much time had passed and too many secrets stayed between them for that.

"I suppose," he finally said as he gazed up at her, "if I force you to leave the country tonight, you won't give up this crazy suicide mission for good."

"You can't force me. And I won't ever give up. We may not be friends anymore, Shakir, but don't make us enemies."

Staring over as though he was seeing right through her, Shakir grazed his knuckles across his mouth. "I'll take you there."

Her heart jumped, ballooning with hope. "Thank you. Thank you. I don't know how I'll ever repay you, but…"

"I don't want your pay—or your thanks. Save them for someone who deserves it. What I do want is your solemn pledge to do exactly as I say. This is a dangerous place and your son is probably in a life-threatening situation."

He stood up and walked toward his pack. "I'll contact my family and ask them to devise a rescue plan while we're traveling through the mountains. If you're willing to follow my instructions, we can make it there in about a week."

"I'm willing. Absolutely. And I swear I'll do everything you say. When can we leave?"

Crouching beside his pack, Shakir turned his face to talk to her. "Fill the canteen and these." He threw her two more collapsible water skins. "We'll leave as soon as I contact my brother."

"Good. But it's not quite dark yet."

Shakir sighed heavily. "*Exactly* as I say, Nicole... Nikki. Exactly. No hesitation. It could mean your life—and the life of your son."

"Right. Sorry." She hurried to fill the water containers.

Each of them might still keep their secrets, but she would follow his instructions to the letter. That is, for long enough to reach her son.

She didn't trust Shakir completely. He hadn't done anything yet to earn her trust. Actually, when she thought back to the past, Shakir had always been hiding something from her. Even as lovers, she'd wondered what he wasn't telling her.

Nikki had grown up a lot in the years since then. Until she learned all his secrets, if she ever did, he would never have her complete trust. But he could be useful for helping her safely through the mountains.

That might not be morally right, and it wasn't anything she would be proud of. But she was dedicated to rescuing her son. Whatever that might entail.

Shakir was still shaken as he used his satellite phone to contact Tarik. "I have no choice but to take her where she wants to go, brother. She's like a trapped wolf that would rather chew its paw off than remain caught in the trap away from its young."

He thought about how impossibly beautiful Nikki had looked in her duress. Telling him the truth had caused her pain. Still the stunning beauty he well remembered, even in her absurd disguise, she nevertheless acted like a totally different person from the woman he'd once known. The woman he'd thought he would never forget.

"You cannot stop a mother in search of her young." He continued with the argument to his brother. "If I take her across the border, she'll just return to face death rather than stay away from Zabbarán. I can't let her do that."

Nikki had once been as fragile as a glass figurine. There had been goodness about her. An openness and an air of political destiny. But now—now she had what seemed like an underlying pool of strength that confused him.

It hurt Shakir, having to think of her being with another man. The idea of her bearing another man's child... He clearly remembered the day she'd sent him away, supposedly in order to do her duty to her country. Learning that she'd had another affair after the arranged marriage fell through had plunged a dagger of regret into his soul.

Tarik tsked at him over the phone. "I've had a feeling this hostage rescue was a bad idea from the start. We didn't know enough to do it right. By the way, brother, our chopper drew small arms fire as we made for the border. The Taj now know for sure a paramilitary team was in their country and that we escaped into Kasht."

"No one was hurt? Do you think the Taj understand that it was a Kadir chopper?"

"No casualties. Everyone's okay. But there's no way of telling if the Taj know who we were for sure."

Tarik exhaled deeply and then went on. "That old woman you forced into coming along with us is frantic. She says the Taj elder, Umar, will not rest until she's returned to him. Claims Umar will send out search parties to scour the country looking for any foreigners to torture in retribution for her kidnapping."

Confused and wary, Shakir said, "Umar is enraged because of her? Why wouldn't he be angrier about losing the women prisoners that meant so much money to him?"

"Apparently the old woman you *rescued* was one of the elder Umar's wives." Tarik's voice almost contained a note of humor. "My guess is you made him look weak in front of the other elders. The old lady herself doesn't seem too unhappy about leaving Zabbarán. But she says she's concerned for the safety of her young friend—she means Nicole."

"Nikki."

"Huh?"

"That's what she's calling herself now, but never mind." Shakir's mind was racing. "We'll be safe enough. But can the old woman help us with information?"

"She says she will try. Meanwhile, we're still working with our covert agents inside Zabbarán. I don't want to lose any of them due to this ill-fated hostage rescue idea of yours."

"Tarik." Shakir's voice shook as he pleaded with his brother to listen. "We must develop a rescue plan for Nikki's son. He's a foreigner and the Taj will not hesitate to torture and kill him merely because he's a baby."

The hum in Tarik's throat was not a good sign. Shakir prepared another argument, hoping to eventually win his point.

At last his brother spoke. "Once again, we don't have all the information we need to pull off a successful rescue. But I agree, we can't sit and do nothing. I'll work on sending someone to scout out the circumstances in Kuh."

Tarik paused, then asked as an afterthought, "You think you can actually make it up there in a week? Even while dragging a woman along?"

Shakir assured his brother that he would have no trouble with the trip to Kuh. He made it sound like a sunshine-filled walk. But in truth, a cold darkness had surrounded him while Tarik talked about the Taj elder seeking retribution by use of torture.

Shakir dug absently at old scars burned deep into the skin of his arms and shoulders, and reminded himself that one could never completely erase one's past. He'd learned all about torture at the hands of his savage warrior grandfather. He knew how to take it and how to inflict it.

But it was the mental scars that scared him the most. If he would be dealing with Taj raiding troops in the mountains, how would he ever keep Nikki from seeing him at his worst moments?

It was much too late to worry about that now. Already obligated and committed to the rescue of her son, Shakir knew he must ignore whatever tender feelings he had left for Nikki. Saving her and her son would take the abilities of a Bedouin warrior—not the gentile efforts of the desert prince she had once thought she'd known.

Gathering up his supplies and strapping a paratrooper-issued Ka-Bar knife to his thigh, Shakir prepared to do battle. Both with Taj soldiers—and with the ghost of a long-ago lost love.

A small band of Taj soldiers arrived at the water well on camelback shortly after sunset. They'd spotted the fresh tracks of two travelers, and their leader had sent out scouts to make an assessment.

The young lieutenant issued orders for a temporary encampment while his scouts determined what kind of person might be walking in the desert without pack animals or guards. He hoped to discover that the foolish travelers were foreigners in Zabbarán.

His orders were clear. Find anyone who may have aided in the kidnap of the elder Umar's wife and theft of his property. And kill the thieves—after making a point of torturing them first.

Torture had its uses, and a small massacre of either the Kasht or of Bedouins wouldn't hurt the lieutenant's chances for promotion. He was more afraid of finding nothing. Like his compatriots in the officers' corps, he was not in the least adverse to the idea of killing and maiming innocents in order to make his mark and please Umar.

"Lieutenant, sir, we are in luck." One of the scouts, his best man in tracking after dark, returned to report. "We've located the tracks of two persons. One of them is wearing sandals belonging to the magnificent elder Umar's household. This smaller person must be either the old wife herself or perhaps one of the woman slaves who were stolen. The other set of tracks we found is far more interesting."

The lieutenant could not imagine how anything would be more exciting than the news that either Umar's wife or one of the escapees they'd been hoping to find was still in Zabbarán. He flicked his wrist to encourage the man to go on.

"The second set of tracks belongs to a big man. A man who wishes to disguise his background. This man wishes to appear as one of our people, but the soles of his shoes tell a different story. The signs say that he is either a foreigner or a Bedouin."

With his mind racing over possibilities, the young lieutenant felt overjoyed. His first real opportunity for advancement within the Taj army would come at the rising of the sun.

Imagining the task ahead would be easy; the ambitious lieutenant couldn't wait to do his worst.

Chapter 5

Nikki followed in Shakir's footsteps as they walked a good distance away from the watering well. They trekked in a north-westerly direction, heading over barren ground toward the towering outline of distant mountains.

Last night the land hadn't seemed so vast. Nor so forbidding. Everywhere she looked the stark gray of sun-bleached rocks stood out in sharp relief against the ochre and tan sands. Small tussocks of sedge grew, God only knew how, amongst the pebbles and small boulders. Nikki couldn't imagine anyone living for long in this unyielding place.

Had she not been so parched, she would've broken down and cried. She would be crying most of all for her son, William. How was her child surviving in this horrid place without her? Did he cry for his *maman* at night?

Nikki couldn't allow herself to dwell on her son's possible circumstances for long or she would end up curled into a useless ball of hysteria. Then she would be good for nothing—least of all for her baby boy.

She wished she could cry, but this county was too darned arid. If she were able to shed real tears instead of silent dry sobs, she would weep over her bad fortune.

Fortune? The word almost made her laugh when she thought of it. Her mother's old saying about making your own fortune came into her mind, reminding her of her sins. It wasn't any sort of nebulous bad luck, but Nikki herself, who'd caused her own problems. She had managed to extinguish the only two bright spots of happiness in her otherwise bland existence—Shakir and William.

She'd stumbled badly as a mother and had managed to lose her son in the process. But long before that disaster, she'd sent Shakir away, knowing full well she would never love another with the same intensity. Both moves were beyond stupid.

If this trip ended in her death, it would only be blind justice. But before she died, she was determined to find her son and see that he left this terrible place.

Knowing it would kill her to keep thinking of William, Nikki tried to put her mind in a better place. To the other good time in her life. Her carefree, young days with Shakir.

She remembered every minute of that time as if it were this morning. One particular stormy afternoon stood out in her memory. The two of them had stolen away for a walk in the fall countryside when the heavens suddenly opened up and drenched them in a cold rain.

They'd raced for shelter, laughing and slipping in the

mud. A warm, empty barn had been the perfect place to wait out the storm. She remembered it all clearly.

As she'd flicked the water from her eyes and shoved back her dripping hair, Shakir had turned her in his arms. His gentle brown eyes became dark in that instant. Brooding and full of challenge. His expression had given her the chills. The sort of chills that can lead to wanting more than one should.

At that moment, if anyone had asked, she would've sworn she could see her destiny in those eyes. And now, as she struggled to put one foot in front of the other across the hot desert sands, misty memories of them together bombarded her mind.

From out of their past, she heard him say, "Nicole." His voice had rippled like warm chocolate under her skin.

Smiling and feeling playful, she'd gone up on tiptoe and licked a drop of water from the corner of his mouth. Instead of a laugh or a lick in return, Shakir had swooped her up in his arms. His powerful kiss had punched her like a bolt of lightning in the tummy. Suddenly the chill in her bones had turned to pure heat, fiery and bold enough to knock her flat.

Shakir had held her upright as he took the kiss deeper, sweeping his tongue into her mouth. The earth had dropped away under her feet as she clung to him.

She could barely feel her extremities, but her core had throbbed with exquisite awareness. Wrapped up in his kiss, in feeling the hard planes of his body pressing into hers, Nicole had hardly noticed when he'd lifted her in his arms. The next thing she knew, he'd gently placed her on a bed of clean straw and was lying beside her.

She'd lost her bearings. And her mind—as she'd found herself tearing at the buttons on his shirt.

Giddy. Dizzy with need, she'd felt frantic to touch his skin. To know the heat, the fire and to experience everything about the strong connection between them.

"Let me." His voice had reverberated through her veins. She would've permitted him anything. Given him everything he wanted.

Tenderly, almost heartbreakingly so, he'd helped her undress and then finished unbuttoning his own shirt, leaving it on but open to allow her access. Next he had slipped off his shoes and slacks and then pulled her into his arms once more.

He was perfect. The sight of him… The magnificence of his nearly naked body had drawn deep sighs from within her chest. She'd wanted him to touch her. Kiss her. Everywhere. She hadn't known how to beg, so she'd reached up and dragged his head down to her breast.

"You're absolutely beautiful, my love." He had taken her hands from his hair and, capturing her wrists in one of his big hands, lifted them above her head. The move had made her breasts arch toward his mouth as her sensitive tips pebbled in anticipation.

She'd felt the beginnings of wet heat between her legs and squirmed under his gaze, wanting—something. With one knee, he'd opened her legs and propped them wide. Not sure what was coming, she had known that whatever it was, bliss would surely follow.

Needing him to help her find the edge, she'd managed enough of a voice to plead. "Please, Shakir. Please."

He'd drawn one of her breasts deep into his mouth and slid his tongue back and forth over the nipple. Fire had raced through her blood as both nipples grew impossibly hard. She'd gasped and arched her back even higher.

Releasing her wrists, he had slid his hands under her hips and blazed kisses down her belly. Her body had tightened, trembling with tension as his tongue explored and lathed.

He'd made love to her with his mouth and with his whispered words of encouragement. Mindless, she'd reached for him, grasping fistfuls of his shirtsleeves, desperate to make him hurry.

"Now." She'd twisted and sobbed, rolling her head from side to side. "Shakir, for God's sake *now.*"

Moving quickly, Shakir had raised his body, hovered above her. "Yes!" He'd thrust into her hard and fast.

Nicole had cried out at the sharp, fleeting pain. She'd been lost in the moment, in the heat, and hadn't expected it. Hadn't prepared.

He'd hesitated, staying perfectly still. "Nicole? Look at me."

She had then did as he asked. Gladly. The pain had receded and her body had already started to become accustomed to the intrusion. But when she'd gazed up into his eyes, she'd found them glazed over in sympathy.

"Don't stop," she gasped.

When he'd begun to ease back from her, she'd wrapped her legs around his hips in an effort to make him stay. The movement had driven him deeper and she'd moaned in appreciation.

The wild sound of her voice had seemed to bring him out of his trancelike state and he'd begun moving again. Picking up his pace, he'd thrusted as she swivelled her hips to meet him move for move. They strained together she'd known nothing this intense, this perfect, could ever happen with anyone else.

Too soon, a wave of heat and rocket blasts of pleasure had shattered violently through her body. At the same moment, Shakir had arched, thrown his head back and shouted to the heavens, following her over that elusive cliff.

Wrapping her arms around his neck, she couldn't help but scream out her release. "Shakir!"

Moving swiftly in the darkness, Shakir checked their surroundings through the NVGs and then swung around, rushing to Nikki's side. He found her eyes glazed, her body rigid.

Taking her by the shoulders and giving them one hard jerk, he tried to make her focus on his face. "What is it? What's wrong?"

"Shakir?" She shook her head and seemed to be steeling herself in order to face whatever terror she'd spotted.

Then she did the strangest thing. She smiled. Not one of the timid or forced smiles she had been giving him ever since he'd first discovered her in Umar's prison. No, this smile was something else entirely. Something he recognized instantly.

He'd seen that satisfied smile on her face before. A long time ago. And he'd dreamed of it many times since. Seeing it now made him go hard.

His gaze raked over her body, making note of the hardened nipples under the rough material covering them. A familiar connection rushed through his body. But instead of doing what came naturally... Instead of backing her up to the nearest boulder and taking her hard and fast, he let his demon furor replace reckless lust.

"What the hell is the matter with you?" His whispered shout was rough, hoarse. "This isn't a game we're playing. Do not yell unless you're in real trouble. Even then, try to gain my attention by any other means besides raising your voice."

The smile disappeared. "I'm sorry. I guess I was sort of daydreaming while we walked."

He knew what she'd been doing. He'd gone off in his head inappropriately on occasion, too. But not when it was a question of life and death. Both of their lives hung by a mere gossamer web, whether she had come to terms with that fact or not.

As Shakir swallowed down his quick flash of anger, he also tried swallowing the idea that it had been his name she'd called out in her daydream. With no real proof he had been the one who starred in her dreams and not her son's father, he wanted to forget what he'd heard. He needed to keep his sense of possession in check where she was concerned. He had no right. She'd sent him away, and he had given her up, turned tail and walked out of her life.

The new moon suddenly came over the mountain peaks and bathed her body in a golden glow. He flipped off the NVGs and studied her again. This time he felt himself drowning in her eyes.

Her face was streaked with dirt, her shoulders slumped with fatigue. Her whole body trembled in the frigid night air. She was exhausted, but her eyes shone brightly as she stared up at him in the moonlight.

As quickly as that flash of desire had appeared in those amber eyes of hers, it was replaced by a flicker full of determination. Slightly on the wild side, her expression also held untamed resolution and something bordering on hysteria. She was starting to lose it. He'd pushed her too far and too fast. They'd already covered the ground he had planned to make for the night. It was time to rest.

After spotting a cave on a high narrow ledge, he helped her climb the basalt cliff to reach it. He left her at the cave's entrance while he checked for traces of wildlife in the vicinity. Knowing that in this desolate mountain range not many four-legged creatures survived to hunt, his first priority was to poke around searching for reptile holes.

Not finding any sign of vipers or spiny-tailed lizards, either outside or inside the cave, was both good and bad news. Good news because Nikki could rest easy in the cave. Bad news because that meant he would have to scout over the ridge, near the next watering hole, for something they could eat.

Their temporary shelter was deep and he led her halfway into the cave and down a side passage before spreading a Mylar blanket on the ground for her. She needed undisturbed sleep most of all. He bunched up a couple of his T-shirts for her to use as a pillow. Then he dug a trench around her and sprinkled it with rubbing alcohol from the first aid kit. If snakes and lizards did come looking for a warm place to rest, they would hesitate before crossing the trench.

He insisted that she drink the rest of the water in her canteen, then walked to the front of the cave, speaking to her over his shoulder. "We can see the foothills for miles from this position. We'll be safe here. In a couple of hours, I'll make for a fresh water spring I know is nearby. Maybe I'll even find something for us to..."

He turned and through his NVGs realized she was already fast asleep. Good. He would rest for a little while, too, and then go hunting.

It might take him some time to complete that first kill of the night. He'd been gone from these inhospitable deserts for many years, and it had been quite some time since he'd needed to slay any prey. His skills were rather rusty.

Shakir spent a few minutes reconnoitring the area surrounding the cave. Nothing stirred. Somewhere in the distance, he heard night carrion as they searched for scraps of meat. The carrion's presence could possibly signal that other humans were somewhere in the vicinity. Not wanting to draw attention to the cave's position, he quickly changed course and headed over the nearest ridge.

In twenty more minutes he'd located the natural spring he remembered from his boyhood. Human prints were clear in the sand below the trickle of water dripping from a crack in the rocks. Bedouins had been here—recently.

He did not fear his ancestors' people. They had raised him, turned him into a man. They would not attack one of their own. But he worried *for* them. A caravan of Bedouins inside Zabbarán these days could mean great trouble. Taj soldiers would not hesitate to murder and maim anyone they found in their path.

Shakir filled his canteen and two more skins. Before he was done, distinct signs of life tickled his senses and caused him to stop, sniff the air. Some other creature was thirsty and coming for the spring water, too.

Quietly, like the sand cat, he climbed the silica-faced chimney above the spring and hunkered down behind a boulder to wait. He was not there long before two desert hares eased out into the clearing in the soft bluish light of dawn.

In the silent language of the ancient desert warrior, Shakir asked for their forgiveness and gave the small creatures great thanks for providing sustenance. "I take only what I must to survive, my neighbors."

As he drew the Ka-Bar, he vowed not to kill the female. For it was taught that she must survive to bring a new generation into the world. But the male would make a good breakfast for Nikki.

Quicker than a blink, the deed was done and Shakir was on his way back to the cave. He singed and dressed the hare before approaching the safety zone near the cave, imagining Nikki would not appreciate seeing her food prepared from scratch in the way of his ancestors.

But when Shakir came close to the clutch of boulders and the ledge nearest the cave, his nose scented something out of place. Smoke. He froze, worried that he'd been too long out of range. Had someone attacked Nikki as she slept? Tried to burn her out of the cave?

Rechecking the air and his instincts, he didn't sense any unknown human activity nearby. But wildfires did not happen by accident in this part of the world. Nothing in nature here would cause natural combustion.

So who could have started a fire without him being able to sense their presence? It made no sense.

He stealthily climbed the basalt, approaching from a

different direction and hoping to sneak up downwind of whoever had started the fire. His body wouldn't move fast enough while his mind raced with worry about Nikki.

She had to be all right. He would not live in a world without her.

The smell of smoke grew stronger the closer he came to the cave's entrance. He flattened himself to the rough surface of the rock and sneaked a peek inside the darkness but could see nothing. In fact, nothing at all seemed out of place and there weren't any visible signs of a smouldering fire. If it hadn't been for that whiff of smoke, no one would've known anything was amiss in their hidden desert shelter.

But Shakir knew. And he worried.

Nikki hesitated with her hand over the heat of the tiny flame. There it was again. A noise. Just a whisper. But it was clear that someone, or something, was in the cave with her.

Damned Shakir, anyway. She'd been stunned to find that he'd really deserted her when she'd awoken all alone in the dark cave. But she should've guessed it would come to something like that. It wasn't as if he hadn't disappeared on her before. This time he might even return.

Perhaps he'd thought he hadn't quite left her defenseless. His pack and the compact assault rifle remained behind. But she didn't have the first idea of how to assemble or fire the weapon. If only he had left her his knife instead. Now *that* she could've used.

Giving her surroundings a quick glance, she decided the backpack might at least give her something to hide behind. The pack was huge—and heavy. When her adrenaline started flowing, maybe she could manage to lift the pack and wield it like a club. She really hoped that wouldn't be necessary. If this intruder was a wild animal, maybe she could scare it off.

"Nikki?" At the sound of Shakir's voice, all the air whooshed out of her lungs.

"Thank God." She fell back and her bottom hit the sand. She stared up at him over the fire as he came close enough to see.

"Who started the fire?"

"Yes, I'm fine and glad to see you, too." Damn him. "Where'd you go?"

He bent down beside the fire and sat back on his haunches. "Later. Who made this fire for you?" He poked around the edges of her fire and blew on it a couple of times to fan the tiny flame.

Of all the nerve. "You left me totally alone and didn't bother to tell me where you were going. I was cold and scared in the dark. I made the fire myself."

"You? Don't be ridiculous. How? With what materials?"

Now he was really getting under her skin. "Do you want a blow-by-blow account? I was hoping you would trust me enough to believe that I was telling the truth."

A strange expression came over his face as he stared at her through the shadows. "I believe you, but I still don't understand."

"I don't understand why you would leave me, either, but…" She sighed, deciding it wasn't worth the effort to argue. "All right. When I woke up—alone—I crawled around until I found your pack and the flashlight I'd seen stashed in the outside pocket. Once I had light, it was pretty easy to get out of the cave. I climbed down the rocks the same way we came up and then found a trail with the materials to build a fire."

When he tilted his head and scowled, she took pity on him. "Before I left to come to Zabbarán, I took a quickie course in desert survival from my neighbor. He teaches at the local college, and…"

"What would he know about surviving in Zabbarán?"

"Desert survival. Deserts are pretty much the same all over the world, aren't they?" It wasn't a real question and she didn't wait for an answer. "He used to be in the French Foreign Legion and originally came from Egypt. A very smart and tough guy."

She eased a couple more of her precious grass sprigs into the fire and watched them catch. "Camel dung. Dry grasses." She shrugged. "Not hard to find. It was harder searching in your backpack for a lighter. Couldn't find one and had to settle for matches."

"I'm impressed."

She could tell that he was more than impressed. He was amazed. She wasn't sure whether to take his accolades with a smile—or if she should smack him over the head for assuming she was still the pampered princess she'd once been.

"Why did you leave? Where did you go?" If she was supposed to be this fragile creature, why had he deserted her?

"We were running out of water. The nearest spring would've been a half day's journey for you. I thought I could make it there and back before you woke up."

"You didn't. But did you bring the water?"

The corners of his mouth cracked up in a form of amusement. "Yes. And I brought something else, too. Breakfast."

Her stomach rumbled at the idea of a croissant covered with soft white cheese. "Great. Let's eat now."

"We have to roast it first." He produced a small skinned animal that looked similar to the rabbits her local butcher hung in his shop. "Good thing you already had the fire going. This shouldn't take too long."

A little later when the meal was over, she decided the meat had been too stringy and tasted gamey. But then, starving people couldn't be choosy and the protein was giving her a whole new outlook on things. When one had strength, everything seemed possible.

Nikki worked on destroying her hard-won fire and tried to make the cave look as though no one had ever been there while Shakir watched their backs. He suddenly stopped at the mouth of their cave, standing as still as the rock beside him.

"What is it?" she asked.

He shook his head and moved back into the cave to whisper in her ear. "Taj soldiers. Close by."

"How do you know it's the Taj?"

Shakir wrinkled up his nose. "I can smell them. Even if they don't find this cave, we still won't be able to get past them without being discovered." He dug out a small handgun from under his belt and vest and handed it to her. "Here. Stay behind the pack and shoot anything that comes into the cave. Except me."

She almost laughed, but kept her expression sober. "What are you planning?"

He turned away from her, and she thought he must

be trying to keep her from seeing his face. "I'm going to take care of it."

Drawing that big knife of his from its sheath, he made a couple more demands. "Stay here. Wait for me."

Before she could say anything, he was gone.

Chapter 6

No chance in the world of her doing that.

Nikki wasn't about to cower in a dark cave, waiting for ferocious soldiers to come torture and kill her. Not in this lifetime, thank you.

She wasn't crazy about carrying the gun, either, but Shakir had shown her how to use it earlier. Hold it with both hands. Keep it low. Press halfway down on the trigger and aim before firing.

A lot to remember. But she stuck the barrel inside her belt and prayed that it wouldn't go off accidently while she carried it. Straightening the kuffiyah disguise on her head, she made her way out into the early morning light.

The heat was not yet oppressive, but Shakir was already out of sight—of course. Nikki looked right and left and then glanced downward toward the base of the cliffs. If she couldn't follow him, then she would have to think like him. Where would he find the soldiers? Where would Taj soldiers rest for the day if they weren't near a cave or a watering hole?

In the shade. And probably close to the trail she'd located last night.

Next, the most important question of all came into her mind. How would she manage to back up Shakir without actually being caught by the soldiers or dying in the effort? She couldn't die. Not yet. Not until she brought William out of Zabbarán.

At that moment a large bird swooped low, sailing on the air drafts above her head and capturing her attention. That was it. She would need to stay high. Up in the rocks where it would be hard for the soldiers to see her.

Feeling smug, she inched her way around the ledge and looked out for any cracks or tiny ledges where she could place her feet. Within moments she realized this expedition wouldn't be so easy. She had to hold on with both hands and watch carefully where she stepped or risk a horrific fall.

Taking a lot of extra care meant it would be difficult to watch out for the soldiers, too. And if she were attacked, she sure as heck wouldn't want to grab for the gun while dangling off the side of a boulder.

Nikki slowed down and took a deep breath. She wasn't about to quit now. Waiting around to either be killed or rescued by a man who kept deserting her wasn't an option. But maybe she should do a little more planning before she ran into bigger trouble.

When raised as a desert warrior, one learned how to track and hunt humans as one would any other animal.

Shakir particularly liked hunting at night. But even in the growing light of day, he was enjoying this hunt. The sun made it more exciting as he tracked the cowardly Taj Zabbar soldiers—men who preyed on those weaker and who shot the strong in the back rather than face them in a fair fight.

He found a set of tracks indicating a squad of four. Four soldiers and one pack mule. He knew exactly which direction they'd been headed. But none of those bastards would reach Nikki. Not while he still drew a breath.

Instinct told him they would've stopped up the trail in the shade of a limestone bluff to rest for the hottest part of the day. But in another few minutes he saw signs that one of them had separated from the others and had gone hunting—probably looking for signs of any strangers. The four-man squad may have even spotted his and Nikki's tracks near the watering hole and knew for sure at least two strangers were in the area.

Shakir was admonishing himself to be more careful with their tracks from now on when he heard one of the soldiers. The man was searching in the high rocks. Shakir waited, judging the prey's proximity by the sounds he made as he huffed down the iron sulphate crevices and then up the smooth shale chutes. In one or two spare movements, Shakir climbed above him and then stepped out onto the ledge as the soldier passed underneath.

Before the soldier knew what happened, Shakir dropped behind him, hooked a forearm around his neck and twisted. Silent. Fast. Lethal. The guy never made a single sound.

Shakir slipped the body down a chute between two boulders and then swivelled around to head back up the trail. He wanted to eliminate the pending threat to Nikki—the entire threat—with no fuss. And he needed to accomplish the task before any of the soldiers could signal to their superiors.

Nikki was exposed high on a trail when she heard a gunshot. Too close. The sound was too close.

She didn't think Shakir would've been firing a gun. He'd been carrying a knife when she saw him last. Even someone as inexperienced as she was knew that it would be bad to have a gunshot echoing around these rocks for anyone to hear.

Jumping down into an indentation between two rocks, she tried to find a way off the trail and into a hiding place. But when she landed off balance, her foot slipped into a crevice and her ankle caught. She tried to lift her foot out of the crack. Then she tried twisting it out. But the more she tugged, the worse her foot seemed to be stuck.

She needed Shakir's help. Was he still alive? How many soldiers had he found? She had a feeling he wouldn't be coming to rescue her anytime soon.

Trembling, she pulled the gun out of her waistband and wedged her back against the rough surface of the boulder behind her. The trail weaved in a tight zigzag pattern around nearby rocks. But she was now stuck in a wide-open spot.

She hefted the gun in both hands and waited. Terrified. Her heart was beating hard enough that she could feel it all the way to her ankle. Her stuck ankle.

Minutes went by. She heard nothing. Her palms were growing sweaty as she grasped the handgun's grip in a death hold.

Her foot was growing numb. How long had it been? Ten minutes? Thirty? What if no one ever came and she was stuck here until she starved or died of thirst?

Then she heard a noise.

Someone was coming. She could hear footsteps against the rocks below as loose pebbles scattered. She held her breath for long minutes, hoping her lungs wouldn't explode.

Then nothing. The footsteps stopped as suddenly as they'd begun.

A slight clunk of a noise, so quiet she might've dreamed it, came next. What was that? It sounded like metal on metal. Like someone drawing and loading a gun?

She swallowed hard and prayed it was Shakir—even knowing that was not the case. He would make no noise. He always traveled like the wind. Silent. Moving like a cat.

Should she call out for his help? No, maybe if she stayed quiet, whoever it was would turn around and miss her entirely.

She sat, trying to make herself as small as possible.

The gun in her hands started to shake. She bit down on her lip, willing her hands to steady—

Suddenly she let out a squeak, sounding for all the world like a trapped mouse, when the silhouette of a man appeared around the bend in the trail.

Not Shakir. A soldier. He raised his rifle and pointed it at her.

She fired. And kept firing until her gun was empty. With her fingers frozen and her mind in shock, she kept depressing the trigger while nothing happened.

"Nikki. It's over." Shakir appeared behind the soldier

sprawled across the trail, reached down and felt the man's neck for a pulse.

Shaking like a leaf in a windstorm, she couldn't lower the gun.

"You're okay. He's dead."

Still terrified, she couldn't move. Shakir stepped over the man's body and lowered himself down to her level.

"Give me the gun." He held out his hand. "Nikki, it's okay."

Finally she dropped the gun and reached out for him. "He…he…"

Shakir wrapped his strong, hard arms around her. "He got away from me. I'm sorry. I took care of the others. This one should've never gotten this far."

She buried her face in his shoulder and wept. "My ankle is stuck. I couldn't hide. He pointed his gun at me. He was going to kill me."

Shakir gathered all his strength to lift the rock pinning her ankle and pull her free. Then he drew her into his arms again and held her close against his chest.

"You did just fine. Nikki? Are you with me? We have to keep moving. Other soldiers will follow when they don't hear from this squad."

Her whole body was shaking violently and she couldn't answer. But she held on.

"I know this was terrible," he whispered in her ear. "But I'm proud of you. The princess I remember would've died here today. But you're alive. Thank God."

She nodded and looked up at him. "I have to save my baby."

He thumbed over her cheeks, drying tears she hadn't

known she was capable of crying. "That's right. But we have to go now. Can you stand? Do you think the ankle is sprained?"

Loosening his grip, he started to lower her to her feet. But she clung to him. His mouth was inches away. His brown eyes full of concern.

Stunned by the sensations rolling over her and suddenly desperate to feel alive, she kissed him. Pouring all her terror and relief into the kiss, she gave him everything. Every ounce of gratitude for coming for her. Every bit of pent up longing and desire that she had secreted away in her heart for years.

Shakir tightened his grip around her and took it all. He returned her kiss with something so full of life and so vital that Nikki knew it was a challenge of sorts.

Stay alive.

When he finally pulled back, he met the questions in her eyes with a wry smile and a look packed with sexual heat. She felt the combustion clear to her toes.

"Perhaps one day…" Then he set her on her feet and straightened his shoulders. "We must go now."

Once she'd gotten the feeling back in her foot, the ankle throbbed whenever she put any weight on it. But as she kept walking, the pain lessened.

As they traveled farther away, she stopped thinking as much about the look on that soldier's face when her bullet had penetrated his chest. She couldn't bear to remember his stunned expression and still go on. So whenever that terrible moment came back to haunt her, she would bring her child's face to mind instead of dwelling on the soldier's.

She had done only what she must in that situation. What she would do again if necessary.

They'd been climbing more on this leg of the journey than they had yesterday. The Taj's pack mule was in tow behind them. The climb was physically demanding work but she was keeping up. Even in the chilled night air, she felt sweaty and smelly and knew the soldier's disguise she wore was filthy enough to stand up on its own.

What she wouldn't give to have a nice warm shower and clean underwear.

Walking ahead of her as the trail evened out, Shakir put his hand out to indicate he was stopping and turned to whisper in her ear. "We're not far from the Bedouins' camp. I need to warn them about Umar's edict and the roving soldiers."

"Okay." She was surprised that he would take the time, but was willing to accept his judgment while they were still on the trail. "Will we rest with them for the daylight hours?"

"These are my mother's people, Nikki. But…" The look in his eyes stopped her cold. Apprehension. Anguish. "But they're nomads—desert warriors. Uh… they're not like anyone you've ever met. I spent my teenage years with them—before I met you. They don't know much about modern conveniences. And they—"

She put her hand on his arm and purred. "They can't be any worse than that horrible Taj elder Umar and his guards. I promise I won't judge them. Or you."

"It's not that," Shakir hedged. "You might be in some danger. You could remain here with a weapon while I go into the camp, but I would rather not leave you alone again."

She didn't want that, either. "Can they do the same

things you can? For instance, since you can feel their camp ahead, do they already know we're here, too?"

"I have little doubt that they've already sensed our presence." He stared at her for a long moment. "You're right. You can't stay behind. But you must not leave my side once we move into the camp. Your disguise will throw them at first, but I'll come up with an explanation. After they learn you're a woman, things will get really touchy."

She didn't like the sound of that. But Shakir seemed willing to take the chance.

He didn't seem willing to do it recklessly, however. He pulled the compact rifle off its place on the pack mule and proceeded to lock the stock into place. Next he loaded the magazine and then tucked the rifle under his arm, ready to pull the trigger at a second's notice.

Nikki swallowed hard at the sight of the desert warrior she saw in him. Six feet four inches of tightly coiled concentration and sheer muscle. With the knife strapped to his thigh and the rifle under his arm, what a picture he made. His swarthy skin and the two days' growth of beard reminded her of the fantasy sheiks of her childhood memories.

A tingle of pure lust rode down her spine. But she knew this was no time to lose self-control. It was merely one more test of her resolve that she needed to pass in order to reach her baby.

Shakir pulled her to his side and enveloped her with his free arm. "Stay close. Don't make a sound. No matter what happens."

He needn't worry. She was glued to him. Not knowing what on earth to expect next, she matched his steps as

they followed the trail around a limestone boulder—
and walked into her destiny.

Shakir wasn't sure his kin would recognize him. He'd
changed a lot in the ten years since he had last traveled
with them.

Before he and Nikki could enter the wide flat mesa
where the nomads were making camp, ten Bedouins
appeared out of the rocks and pointed weapons straight
at their hearts. He called out a greeting in their language.
That seemed to confuse the warrior guards because so
few outsiders ever learned the true language of the desert.

"What do you want?" one of them asked carefully.

"I have come to trade." Trade was the only thing
besides armed conflict that the Bedouin respected. "I
wish to trade with your sheik for safe passage beyond
your camp."

Despite giving Nikki and the mule a few narrowed
and disparaging looks, the warriors lowered their rifles
and placed them loosely in the crook of their arms the
same way he carried the one at his side. Then the armed
warriors showed the travelers into their camp.

After they'd walked past several smaller tents, the
whole group arrived at what Shakir recognized as an
elder's tent. "We've got a little problem," he whispered to
Nikki, letting no one else hear. "You must not enter this
tent. It's men only. And I can't leave you alone outside
with the mule."

"What'll we do?"

"I have an idea. Say nothing." He sure hoped he was
betting right. Surprise usually trumped mild irritation
when one was in a tight situation.

He stood at the tent's entrance and called out in Bedouin, "I address my cousins, the Bedouin princes of the desert. I walk in your trail and drink from your well for the first time in many years."

Shakir checked his peripheral vision and was grateful to see a crowd gathering. He twisted his arm around and in one flamboyant move pulled the soldier's kuffiyah off Nikki's head. A thick fall of her honey-blond hair cascaded down to her shoulders. The crowd gasped.

"I have brought my first wife to introduce to my cousins. And I come to trade information for passage."

Standing in the open air in the dawn's growing light and yelling as though one was screaming war whoops was considered quite impolite in Bedouin society. But Shakir thought if he could bring the elders outside, he and Nikki might have a better chance of leaving here alive.

All he needed was for one elder's curiosity to get the better of him and bring him out.

No movement from inside the tent. Not even a whisper of a breeze stirred the flimsy covering over the entrance.

Shakir wished he had something else to trade. Something flashy. Then it hit him. He did have something.

Digging into his vest pocket, he pulled out his butane lighter. Saying nothing, he reached down and picked up the head scarf that Nikki had been wearing.

With as much flourish as he could muster, he held both the scarf and the lighter high above his head and then flicked the lighter to life. These people were used to matches, though they didn't get their hands on them every day. But the quick flash of flame from his hand drew their united attention. Every eye was on him as he lit the scarf and it burned brightly.

"Very amusing, cousin. Entertaining the savages?" A man about his own age appeared at the tent's entrance and spoke in English.

Shakir dropped his hands and extinguished the fire. Then he looked over at his second cousin as a broad smile broke out on his face.

"Kalil?" He could scarcely believe his eyes. The young warrior he'd ridden with and who'd taught him how to hunt and fight in his youth now wore the robes of the sheik, a prince of the desert.

Kalil put a hand on his forearm. "Welcome to the camp of your ancestors, Shakir." His gaze raked over Shakir's T-shirt and black pants and then flicked toward Nikki. "I think there must be an interesting story that accompanies you this day."

Shakir introduced Nikki and then said, "I have information to trade, Kalil. But first, my woman is in need of rest. May she sit in the female tent?"

"She looks in need of more than rest. And that Taj soldier's uniform offends me." Kalil snapped his fingers and two women appeared out of the crowd. "We will provide you both with hospitality and enough water for your animal. But first you must bring me up-to-date."

Shakir turned to Nikki. "I don't know what languages they speak besides Bedouin. Do you think you can communicate with the women?"

Nikki flipped a flyaway strand of hair back off her forehead and glared at him. "Don't worry about me. We *women* have a language all our own."

"Would you like a bath and a change to more appropriate clothing, madame?" one of the Bedouin women asked politely in French.

Nikki's eyes lit up like fireworks. She threw a sarcastic look back at Shakir as she put an arm around the old woman's shoulders. "You go do your man things, Shakir. I'm just fine."

Watching her walk away swinging those curvy hips, he chuckled to himself. Yeah, she was fine all right. Very, very fine. And all his thoughts were becoming very, very bad.

Chapter 7

When the reckless and selfish Bedouin youth named Matin spotted the odd-looking woman's honey-gold hair, greed quickly replaced his shock. He'd been suffering for a long time. Everything was against him. Even the small goats his clan had used for trading were gone. They'd been casualties of the lack of grass for feed.

Kalil had explained to him the reason for not finding enough grazing spots this year. He'd said it was because the Taj had planted poppies in a nearby valley and then diverted the precious water needed to make even meager grass grow. But Matin wasn't sure about that reasoning. What did plants have to do with water from the mountains?

At times it seemed as though he must be cursed. Bad luck shadowed him like a dark cloud. He needed a chance to make his own luck for a change. He deserved a break.

A beautiful woman like the one with honey-colored hair could be the chance he needed. She would be useful as barter. Matin had heard rumors about the Taj buying women as wives. He knew little of the ways of other peoples, but his tribe had crossed into the land of the Taj many days ago. It was also said the Taj had gold. Gold and goods.

Matin knew he was not strong enough to force the honey-haired woman from her warrior protector. The male Kalil had addressed as *Shakir* was too tall, too broad and too healthy for Matin to fight. But perhaps the Taj Zabbar might still be willing to trade a little gold for information.

He checked over his shoulder to make sure no one was watching and then sneaked behind the elders' tent. Lowering himself to the sand and crawling low, Matin searched for a good spot to listen. If he could get close enough, perhaps he would hear something useful. Something to trade.

"I appreciate your warnings, cousin, but I wonder where you are planning to travel from here?" Kalil's voice was low, easy, though Matin could clearly hear his words. "If strangers to the Taj are in danger here, why did you not leave Zabbarán at the first opportunity?"

"I cannot leave until my woman and I retrieve the son that was stolen from her." The stranger called Shakir also spoke in an easy tone. "I am her protector. Her shadow—until the day the sun shines for her once again. Where she goes, I go."

"Her son. But not your son. Then she is not your first wife?"

"No," the whispered answer was almost too low for

Matin to hear. "But she and her son are my charges, Kalil. At least until we can leave Zabbarán."

"Do you know where to look for this boy?"

"She has been told he is in the small valley town below the mountain that the Bedouin call Al Dia-Attuh."

"Ah. But that is many days' walk, following the setting sun and across rough terrain if you wish to travel the fastest route."

"That is so. But it is a journey of her heart. We must go."

"I would offer a suggestion, cousin. Horses could make your journey quicker."

"As you can see, my prince, we have no horses. But that's a fine suggestion." The stranger chuckled and Kalil offered him a cup of cardamom coffee.

Young Matin decided he had heard enough. It was time for him to make a strategic retreat before someone caught him listening.

But he now had a piece of information that could be worthwhile to the Taj. He knew where the stranger and the beauty were headed. He hoped the Taj were in a generous mood.

Matin was sure the Taj would kill the tall warrior stranger if they could catch him. But Matin would not let concern for another family's son stop him from making a trade. He had needs.

Nikki stretched and came awake, reclining on a bed of blankets. She felt rested and clean. The Bedouin women had allowed her to use a bowl of their precious well water to wash, and then offered her one of their own dresses to wear. It was amazing how much better a situation could seem with warm water, fresh clothes and eight hours of sleep.

Lying flat on her back and easing herself awake, she noticed it was too warm in the small tent where she'd fallen asleep. Too warm and too claustrophobic. Earlier, her hostess had shown her to this place and said the tiny tent belonged to a newly married couple who'd given permission for her to rest for the day.

A bit blurry-eyed, Nikki was surprised that she could still see in the dim light of the tent. She wondered that dusk had not arrived yet. It seemed as if she'd slept forever.

"You're awake." Shakir's deep voice threw her into a minor panic as she rose up on her elbows and looked over at him. "Are you hungry?" he asked casually.

His voice sounded so steady that she relaxed. "What are you doing in here? I thought the women and men stayed in different tents. Will you upset the sheik?"

"This tent is made for a resting couple. The sheik offered to let us use it."

"Did you sleep here?" Next to her? Nikki didn't know how she felt about that. They'd been a couple once, but they had destroyed that relationship. What would she do if he offered her a chance to change history?

"For a few hours," he replied. "But I'm well rested and ready to leave this place. The Bedouin tribe will be moving out after dark. They've offered to share their meager meal with us first."

"Are they leaving because of the Taj?" Nikki hoped it wasn't because of her coming to their camp. She would hate to be the cause of such turmoil to the people who had been this kind to them.

Shakir reached over and used his fingertips to smooth

out the frown lines on her forehead. "The sheik does have some concern about his tribe being fit enough to do battle with the Taj. They grow weaker without the protein they normally eat. But his bigger concern is the lack of grasses on this mesa. None of their sheep will survive if they don't move on soon."

"Will they leave Zabbarán?"

Shakir nodded. "I have offered them the pack mule to make their journey easier. But I think they might eat the scrawny thing before they reach their next grazing land."

Nikki shivered in the heat. "I don't want to hear about it."

Shakir gave her one of his trademark self-depreciating grins and his eyes became that gooey chocolate mixture of concern and sexual interest again. "Nomad life is bloody hard, Nik. Desert peoples must contend with many things you might not want to hear about in order for them to survive. But these Bedouin tribesmen are my mother's kin. I…uh…spent much of my childhood living in their tents."

He'd made that statement as if he were ashamed of his childhood—and these people. But why? Just because people were different didn't mean they were somehow less.

She thought if she asked him to talk about his childhood experiences, maybe he would explain what was going on behind that odd expression on his face. Most of the time he looked like he would like to eat her for supper. She knew the feeling well. She'd felt it herself more than once.

But every now and then, the expression in his eyes made it seem as if he was slightly afraid of her. Not afraid *for* her as she'd originally thought, but afraid *of* her. Her? She was a good nine or ten inches shorter and maybe eighty pounds lighter. What on earth was going on in the man's head?

Nothing about him was simple.

"We have a little time before supper," she said softly. "Tell me about your childhood. We never spoke of it—before."

Shakir palmed her cheek with a touch so soft she was reminded of the silken baby powder she'd used on William. But Shakir had barely touched her before the electricity began rippling along the skin on her arms. She felt a sudden breathlessness, and a heat far stronger than the desert sun.

His eyes filled with sensuality as she tried to avoid his gaze. The palms of her hands tingled. Her breasts felt sensitive and ached. Her pulse raced.

Her body was sliding away from her and her control was slipping into oblivion. Worse, he knew what his touch was doing to her.

Swallowing hard, she tried to slow them both down by asking again. "Talk to me, Shakir. Since we can't leave yet, I want to know more about you."

He pulled his hand back, fisted it and shook his head. "There's nothing much to tell."

"I disagree. Start at the beginning. You have two brothers…"

"Yes," he said reluctantly. "One older and one younger. Darin is older. And you met my younger brother, Tarik, when we brought you and the other women out of Umar's fortress. Tarik likes to think he's smarter and tougher than the rest of us in the family. But the truth is he's a chameleon. He learned from an early age how to put on an act, become whoever he wanted to become." Shakir's voice wound down as he finished telling the story of his brother.

She needed to keep him talking and not tempted to do other things. "Your mother died when you three boys were still children, isn't that right?"

Shakir would rather not talk about himself. But he understood what she was doing. Trying to take their minds off finding themselves together—alone with nothing to do for a half hour before they could be on their way again. In their distant past, any stray free moments had always been filled with touching, with tasting and with learning each other's desires.

He remembered it all too well. Not enough time could ever go by to make him forget that she had loved to have the back of her neck kissed. And the inside of her thighs stroked.

But those kinds of thoughts now would only lead them into a situation neither of them could afford. In addition to that, she needed to better understand what kind of man he was before he ever touched her again.

Perhaps this was as good a time as any. "Yes," he reluctantly answered. "I was ten when my mother died. Darin was fourteen and Tarik was five years old."

"That must have been hard on all of you." She reached out to push a stray strand of hair off his forehead.

Shakir inhaled deeply. "You have no idea. Our father is…dedicated to the Kadirs' business interests. He spent the first few years wallowing in his own grief at the loss of his wife. Rather than face reality, our father simply abandoned us to be raised by employees until each of us was old enough to leave home for our education."

"I was also raised by employees," Nikki told him sympathetically. "Nannies and housekeepers. I know how hard that can be. I'm sorry."

He didn't want her pity, but he also felt compelled to tell her the truth. "Darin left home for boarding school in the U.S. almost immediately. I was at a loss without both my big brother and my parents. It affected me deeply. I ended up with a difficult stutter."

"Your voice? Really? I've never noticed any problems. How did you find a cure?"

"There is no cure, Nik. But with self-control and practice it can be conquered. Even now I have to think about my speech every time I open my mouth. As a boy my father sent me to specialists all over the world, but it was my mother's father who made the biggest difference."

"How can that be? Didn't you say that your grandfather was a member of this Bedouin tribe?"

"I did, and he was. My grandfather was their sheik, the leader of this tribe before his death a few years ago. His preference would've been for all of his grandsons to abandon the Kadir family after our mother's death and join his tribe. He insisted that each of us must learn to become his version of adult men. But my father would only send me—the one that caused him the most concern."

"Because of the stuttering?"

Shakir screwed up his mouth and glanced away for a second, not willing to look at her as he told his story. "Yes. And my grandfather assured my father that he knew of a cure."

"But you said…"

He turned around to face her rather than be a coward.

"That there is no true cure. Right. But my grandfather had a plan." The memories suddenly swamped Shakir and he had to swallow hard and force them back.

"Uh…" Nikki put her hand to her mouth. "I don't like the look on your face—as though it's painful to think of the old times. Don't tell me. Think of something else. Can't we leave now?"

He softened his voice. "You know we must wait. But memories shouldn't hurt people. Only people can hurt people. My grandfather loved me, I know he did. But he didn't believe that physical pain was a bad thing. To him, experiencing pain was what made men brave and clearheaded."

Hesitating for only a moment, Shakir decided it was time for Nikki to understand. She had never seen him without long sleeves or completely naked. He'd been careful not to make it seem like a big deal. But now she must see what he had hidden from her and from everyone in the past, even if it meant that the two of them could never again be close. He unbuttoned the soft white linen shirt that Kalil had loaned him to wear and slid his arms free of the long sleeves.

"Oh, my God." Nikki gasped and put her hands to her eyes as if she would blot out the sight. "Why didn't I already know those scars were there? Is this why you never completely disrobed when we were together?"

She exhaled and then gazed at him with questions in her eyes. "Your grandfather did this to you. How could he?"

"These scars are nothing that he would not have done to any of the other young men in his tribe." Shakir stared down at his own arms. At the hundreds of burn marks and knife wound scars. It wasn't a pretty sight.

"Even Kalil has a few of these same scars," he added. "Each young man must experience the pain and earn his own scars. These are marks designating the changeover time when a youth becomes a man of the tribe. It makes us all more brothers than cousins."

"This many scars? Do all the men in the tribe look the same?"

"Not exactly the same. I was different. Special. I was given a new mark for every time I slipped up and stuttered. My grandfather believed that as my will grew stronger through the pain, I would be better able to fight off my affliction. He was right."

Nikki placed her fingers against the deep gashes, touching each as if she could heal them with the power of her mind. Her touch was gentle, empathetic and— sensual.

Shakir could barely fathom how often he had dreamed of her touching him just this way. Hundreds of times at least. Perhaps millions.

Once he would've given anything for her to look past the ugliness and find the man underneath. But he had never given her that chance. Now that she was living his dream, he knew he could not let her continue. This was not the place and it was not yet their hour.

She still didn't comprehend what kind of a man he really was. What he was capable of doing. To her, these marks were only the outward signs of what had been inflicted upon him. She did not understand that to survive these wounds, this place, he'd had to become as ruthless as his grandfather. She had no way of knowing what a savage nature lurked beneath his more civilized, British-trained exterior.

Capturing her fingers with his hands to hold them

still, he said, "We must go. We'll join the tribe for a light meal and then be on our way. Tonight's journey is a difficult one and I want to be miles farther up in the mountains before nightfall."

She tilted her head, stared him right in the eyes and then sighed. "You're right. We have to reach my son. Soon. We can't let ourselves be sidetracked."

She stood and reached for a black, rectangular scarf like the ones used by Bedouin women. "Will you help me with this?"

He studied her in the soft light. She was clothed in one of the loose, unencumbered dresses of the Bedouin women in this tribe. It was midnight-blue with wide sleeves and a sash tied around the hips. Except for her coloring, Nikki could've easily passed for a wife of one of the desert dwellers.

Helping her wrap the head scarf around and under her chin, he could see the determined spirit in her eyes and knew her thoughts were all for her son. But as they picked up their things and moved out of the tent, Shakir wished they'd been granted a little time of their own. Time enough for two people to let go, become sidetracked and live their dreams together once again.

"Where are we headed?" Nikki sneaked a peek at her compass in the late afternoon light. They weren't on the same course as before they'd stopped at the Bedouin's camp.

"We're taking a slight detour."

"What? But why? This climb is already so hard that we'll never make it to the other side in the time you promised your brother. Even going a few miles out of our way is too much." She was tired enough now that she could barely put one foot in front of the other.

"In the first place," Shakir said from over his shoulder, "I'll contact my brother when we reach the other side of the range. As soon as we're within a few hours of the town of Kuh Friez. If we're late, Tarik will use the time to do a more thorough assessment of our chances."

Shakir stopped, held up his hand and then turned back to her. "In the second place, you'll thank me for this detour."

"Why? What's up ahead?" She had visions of an oasis spa. With mineral baths and a foot massage.

"It's one of the Taj Zabbar's far-flung military outposts."

"Are you crazy? We can't go there. They'll capture us. Maybe even kill us."

Shakir tilted his head. "First they have to know we're around. Kalil gave me a secret way to sneak into their camp without them being any the wiser."

"It's still a crazy idea. Why on earth would we want to sneak into the place? I don't want to be within ten miles of Taj soldiers."

"You'll change your mind when you hear what we're planning to do at this outpost."

He was being deliberately obtuse and annoying. Her feet hurt too much to put up with him.

"All right. What are we planning on doing?"

"This outpost is used to replenish the troops. With food and supplies. And with fresh pack mules and mounts."

"You're not planning on stealing their food are you?"

He'd better not be. Her life and the life of her son

were far more important than their taste buds. They should continue eating whatever he could catch in the wild.

"Nope," he told her as his eyes lit with amusement. "You and I are crossing the rest of this mountain range in style—after we steal a couple of Taj horses."

Oh, for heaven's sake. Couldn't he have asked her first?

"On horseback? I can't." She threw up her hands. "I've never been on a horse. I don't know how to ride."

Chapter 8

It took a lot of talking, but Shakir finally convinced Nikki that she could learn enough about riding in a few minutes to remain on the back of a horse as they crossed the mountains. While he'd argued his case, they kept heading in the direction of the Taj outpost.

She hadn't said so, but he believed she was afraid of the horses. Once upon a time, he might've considered that a good possibility where Princess Nicole of Olianberg was concerned. But the thought of Nikki Olivier being afraid of anything never would've occurred to him after he'd seen her shoot a man to death. The more he heard her shaky arguments against using the horses, however, the more he felt he was right.

It was beyond him how a woman who'd had the nerve to come all the way to a distant and dangerous land, and who'd had no trouble heading off across a forbidding desert alone, could possibly be afraid of a domesticated animal. But Shakir wasn't going to let a case of simple nerves stop them.

Twilight arrived across the land just as they entered the far end of the deep gorge that Kalil had promised would lead them to a spot below the horse stables. They'd climbed high enough in the foothills that they still had an hour of daylight left to make the trip.

Nikki was dressed in the same midnight-blue dress as before, and he wore the typical Bedouin male's rust-colored and belted wool shawl covering his white linen shirt. That, along with his camo backpack, would allow them to blend in with the growing shadows on the stark and barren land, making them almost invisible.

After fifteen minutes of hard walking, he leaned in close and whispered, "This is the place. I'll help you take the first few steps up."

She looked from him to the sheer wall of the cliff beside them and her eyes grew wide. "No way."

It wasn't fear he saw in those fantastic hazel eyes this time. No, not fear, but disappointment mixed with an odd determination.

"You go first," she said before he could suggest it.

Nodding his agreement, he slipped the ten-foot long wool scarf out of his belt. He tied one end around her waist and the other to his own.

"Stay in my footsteps." He turned, grabbed for a stringy saltbush and jerked it hard. When it held, he used it to hoist his body up to the first foothold in the rocks.

Nikki scrambled up right behind him, looking more like a mountain goat than a beautiful woman with robes flowing out around her. Silently, they made the climb.

Then, together at the rim, they untied the scarf and peered over the edge.

The horses weren't far away in an open paddock with a wooden fence. He could see about a half dozen trail horses grazing there. But Kalil had forgotten to mention that the path from the paddock to the gorge was a wide open space. Several outbuildings were scattered about the area; a hay barn, a square building that appeared to be for storage and even a long, tin-sided building that might be furnished with extra stalls or solar-style showers. Perhaps if the two of them ducked behind each of those buildings one at a time, they would be able to circle around and come closer to the paddock without being exposed.

"Stay with me. We're taking the long way. Ready?"

Nikki nodded.

Without another word, Shakir took her by the hand and they scrambled over the rim of the gorge and ran full-out for the nearby hay barn. Out of breath beside the barn, Shakir crouched low and checked the area for any signs of life.

Except for the horses gently swishing their tails and chewing on the tuffs of sedge in their grass paddock, nothing stirred. It seemed too quiet. He wondered if it could be mealtime. Lifting his eyes to a building in the distance that might be used as a dining hall or mess, he saw a single light.

He didn't like the feel of the situation here.

All of a sudden chaos exploded out of the quiet evening. A squad of soldiers on horseback rode onto the mesa from the south. A monsoon of dust rose around the dozen men as they slowed their mounts to a walk. Shakir was sure they were headed right for them.

"We have to move," he whispered to Nikki. "They'll be here at the barn or in the paddock within minutes, and they'll see us if we stay too long."

"But we can't go back. It's too open in the direction of the gorge."

Shakir quickly decided on a Plan B. "The storage building. It doesn't look like anyone's used it in months. And it's out of their line of sight. We can make it."

But they had to go now. Staying low, he practically crawled on all fours to reach the far side of the squat, square building where a door was located. Nikki kept right beside him.

When they reached the door, he wasn't surprised to find it padlocked with an old metal lock. Using the butt end of his rifle to break through the rust, he pushed the door open on squeaky hinges. He shoved Nikki inside and followed her into the darkness. Easing the door shut behind them, he prayed no one would come around to this side of the building to notice the lock was broken open until after the two of them were long gone.

One lone window, directly opposite the door, was covered in dust and dirt. No one could see in or out, but some light filtered through. Once his eyes became accustomed to the lower level of light inside the one square room, he could see what the Taj had been storing.

Half the space was taken up with tack; saddles, blankets and bridles—most of which looked in need of repair. On the other side of the room sat stacks of various-size boxes. Some were marked as medical supplies and food stuffs, others as ammunition. It seemed an odd combination until he realized every box was out-of-date by at least a year.

Since they hadn't gotten rid of the stuff, Shakir imagined they were holding on to the out-of-date items in case of emergencies. If soldiers were starving or being attacked, they wouldn't much care if the supplies might kill them first.

Shakir realized he needed to get Nikki settled fast. Rummaging through the frayed blankets, he checked each one over for fleas or mites. Once satisfied that they wouldn't be worse off, he fashioned a sort of nest that was big enough for the two of them. Then he placed it directly under the window so as to hear what was going on outside.

They hunkered down just in time. Sounds of arriving horses and men approached, stopping nearby the storage building. Shakir didn't need to see them to visualize what was happening.

The men had been on the trail for a while and they and their horses needed rest. Orders were shouted out for men to feed, water and groom the horses before anyone refreshed themselves.

"What's going on?" Nikki could hear the men but Shakir knew she didn't understand the language.

"They'll be a while. But we can…" Suddenly two of the voices came closer to their window. Shakir put his finger to his lips and Nikki nodded that she understood.

A deep male voice was saying, "Yes, Captain. We encountered one Bedouin who we tortured and killed as instructed. He was no trouble. Only a naïve youth who thought he could sell Taj Zabbar soldiers information."

The men outside the window laughed as though

they'd heard a great joke. Shakir had to fight his rage. They talked too easily about killing. He killed whenever necessary. But he never treated it casually.

"What information?" The second male voice was firmer, a man in command.

"The boy said his tribe had given shelter to strangers. One, a big male who looked like he was one of the Bedouins, and the other a woman with honey-colored hair."

"Before he died, did you get him to tell you where the Bedouin tribe was camped?"

The reply to that question was spoken too quietly to hear, but the next statement from the captain came loud and clear. "As soon as the horses are fed and rested, we ride. At daybreak if not before. Have no fear. We'll encounter little trouble catching up to a slow-moving Bedouin tribe with women and children."

Shakir was grateful that Nikki couldn't understand what had been said. He hoped Kalil and his tribe had enough of a head start to beat these soldiers to the border. Then he remembered that Kalil as a teen had been a genius at negotiating rock trails and blind canyons. If anyone could hide a camp full of women, children and sheep from the Taj, it would be Kalil.

After a few more sharply issued instructions, the two officers' voices drifted away from the window. The captain ordered a few of the men to stay at the barn with the horses and the others to leave for the dining tent for their food and rest.

Shakir drew his first breath since sitting under the window and shrugged out of his pack.

"What did you hear? Are they leaving so we can get out of here?" Nikki was smart enough to know the two soldiers had moved on and weren't close enough to hear them talking anymore.

Just then a bright light exploded through the window. Nikki gasped and put her hand over her mouth.

"Take it easy," he said soothingly. "I suspect they're lighting torches or a few lanterns outside the hay barn in order to see the horses while they work. There's no electricity and the soldiers will only need to see well enough to groom their stock. Most of the men are already leaving for chow."

Nikki's shoulders relaxed and she blew out a breath. "How long will anyone be out there?"

Her face was a picture of determination. Her eyes burned with their own kind of ruthless fire. He watched her chest heave as she attempted to even her breathing and calm down.

Looking at her made him suddenly hungry to see more. To strip her naked and feel all that willpower under his fingers. To lose himself in her fire and in the glory that he well remembered.

"A couple of hours. No more." Forcing his gaze away from the temptation, he leaned back and used his pack as a pillow, trying to put a few more feet of safety between the two of them. He had no right to want her this much.

"Promise?" The look on her face told him the word was a joke—that she understood he didn't know any more than she did about when they'd be able to leave.

But he still heard the underlying concern and knew any delay meant that much more time away from her son. Without her saying as much, he was beginning to understand that each additional hour she had to spend in Zabbarán without her boy was driving her mad. She had seen for herself now how harsh the land could be. And how ruthless the people who lived here were.

The idea of her child facing such conditions without her being able to help him was causing Nikki to worry more and more about the boy's welfare. When she'd first arrived in Zabbarán, before being taken prisoner, she must've thought her son was in a pleasant environment. With people who'd wanted him and would love him. Now she was slowly learning the awful truth, but she didn't want to face those possibilities.

Though Shakir could see all of that in her face, he didn't know how to make a difference. How to make the horror go away. He knew how much effort it took to hide one's true feelings. He'd been doing it for most of his life.

A horse would take at least a day off their trip. It would've been his gift—the least and the most he could do. Now they were stuck here, spending precious hours and all he could give her was lust.

He should be ashamed on many levels. But nothing he said to himself seemed to make a difference. He wanted her as he had always wanted her. Perhaps more.

Nikki unwound the scarf from her head and let her lush hair fall loose to her shoulders. "The time seems to be crawling by. I may go nuts waiting." He knew she was counting the seconds but was trying not to whine.

She started to lean back against the mountain of horse blankets, but sat up again quickly. "Ow. Something hurts."

"Where? What? Let me see."

"My shoulder." She turned around and in the dim light he could see her dress was torn and blood was seeping out of the opening in the material.

"You're injured. Do you remember how it happened?"

"No. All this heavy material kept getting caught on the rocks and bushes on the way up the cliff. I didn't want anything to slow us down so I ignored it."

"A wound could easily become infected in the wild, Nik. You can't leave it open like that. I have to see it—treat it."

She nodded sharply, then obediently slipped off the belt and reached for the hem of her dress. With his help on the side with the wound, she pulled the heavy material up and over her head.

Which left her clothed in nothing but a slightly worse-for-wear pink bra and panties. The undergarments might not be new, but they sent heat scorching through Shakir's veins. The sight of her pale, creamy skin was more than he could take right now.

He tried not to look. But he was bound to see everything when he checked the wound. He didn't want to touch her skin. But he would be forced to touch her in order to help.

Who would help him? Who could erase the sensual sights before him, or eliminate the lust-filled memories bombarding his mind?

He cleared his throat. "The wound isn't deep, but the edges are jagged. A butterfly bandage should do the trick."

"I'm glad to know I'm not dying."

"Hmm." He ripped open an antibiotic wipe from his pack. "Hold still. This may sting a little."

She made no sound at all, but her eyes squeezed shut in response.

After cleaning it thoroughly and putting antibiotic

salve on the wound, he drew the edges together with a bandage from his medicine kit. Leaning back, he inspected his work.

"That should hold." It was only then that he noticed her eyes were tightly shut. "Still hurts?"

"Yes, a lot. That is, unless one enjoys pain the way some people I know do." She gave him a wounded smile and he knew she was teasing.

But he wished like hell that he could take her pain into himself. It killed him that she was suffering. He'd come to Zabbarán on this rescue mission to keep her safe. Some job he was doing on that account.

"Oh, don't make such a face," she said with a chuckle. "It was just a joke."

She rose up on her knees, put her hands on either side of his face and kissed him. Her lips were gentle, warm, as she settled against him. He was the one who turned the kiss to something else entirely.

He could no more stop what was happening than he could walk away from her. Holding her head steady with one hand, he deepened their kiss. His tongue swept into her mouth with an urgency his whole body was feeling.

She murmured her approval, dropped her hands and flattened her warm palms on his chest. He wanted her and another chance to make love to her after years of thirsting for her touch. He wanted everything.

Knowing full well he was not entitled to have forever, he settled for taking what was offered right now. With his body growing hard, he fought his savage nature and tried to slow things down. This was a moment to experience. To savor. The circumstances may not be ideal, but he could give her this. A few minutes to stop thinking and let herself feel.

Without breaking the kiss, he flattened his palm on her bare stomach and felt her quivering. Her skin felt like cool silk beneath his fingertips. He watched her pulse thrum at the base of her neck. She arched her back, and he slid his hand upward to cover one jutting nipple. Instantly, deliciously, she pebbled against his palm.

Breaking the kiss, he whispered, "I'd almost forgotten how responsive you are. How sweet."

He shoved the bra away and flicked his tongue over the hardened tip. Kissing the underside of her breasts, he nibbled his way down to her stomach. Laving, lapping, nipping, he worshipped her—both body and spirit.

She reached for his shoulders as he slid his fingers underneath the waistband of her panties. Heat, wet and seductive, greeted him as he slipped his fingers inside.

Whimpering his name, she buried her hands in his hair. He tried to silence her by covering her mouth with his own, but soon found himself groaning with frustration at the slow pace he had set. She began to pant as his fingers slid deeper, and he had to swallow her tiny moans.

Swollen and slick and ready. Her internal canal clenched around his fingers and she rammed hard against his hand. For one second his brain fried with intense memories of times past.

Old realities mixed with new, and lost years crumbled to dust as she sat up, clinging to him. He was thrown back to another time. A softer time.

Her hands moved to his zipper and freed his erection, then her fingers closed around him. But he was too close to allow her the freedom. It had been too long for him.

He tried steady breathing and took her hands in his. The moment he inched away, she slithered out of her panties and reached to touch him intimately again.

Utterly uninhibited, she looked up at him. "Please." The word was soft, breathless. "Come inside me, Shakir. I've wanted you for so long."

"Easy, love." Laying her back against the hay, he covered her with his body. Oh, how he had missed this. Missed her. Her vital strength. Her soft curves nestled against his hard body.

The brutal beast within him rose dangerously close to the surface. He checked his natural tendencies by the sheer power of his will.

As he parted her legs with his knee, her breath caught on a throaty gasp. He couldn't resist running his palms up the inside of her satin thighs, knowing it drove her wild. She thrashed and pleaded, raising her hips provocatively.

"Now," she sobbed as echoes of the past shimmered into his present.

"Shh, my love," he whispered against her ear. "They must not hear."

She widened her eyes at that and he used the opportunity to press inside her waiting body. Man seeking woman. The way of destiny. Her body gloved him as he thrust home.

As if on cue, her eyes fluttered shut and an expression of pure bliss spread across her face.

"Open your eyes, Nik." He eased up on his elbows and held her head steady.

She obeyed and her eyes latched on to his in a

bold gaze. He watched the building passion turn her hazel eyes stormy green. Then he saw the determined concentration on her face cloud over with desire.

As she gave herself up to his safekeeping, he set the pace, all the while fighting his dark, animal side. But both of them had been too long away from the opposite sex. Within minutes they hit a roller-coaster ride, free-falling together as he filled her with everything he had. His heart and his spirit freely given. Heart to pounding heart, they tumbled as one over that glorious edge into oblivion.

Trying to calm her jackhammering pulse rate, Nikki gulped in breaths of air and clung to Shakir.

When she could finally speak, her voice was a raspy, whispery disaster. "I'd never forgotten for one day how wonderful it feels to have you inside me. Not for one second."

He raised his head and stared down at her. "This was a mistake."

That wasn't what she wanted to hear. Not now when every cell in her body craved words of love.

Rolling off her, Shakir found the discarded Bedouin dress and held it out. "Let me help you get dressed. We need to listen and pay attention. The soldiers shouldn't be in the paddock with the horses much longer. We have to be ready to move."

With a sated body but a bruised ego, Nikki slipped the heavy material over her head and retied the belt at her hips. How could he treat their lovemaking so cavalierly? She felt sure that it had meant something to him. His eyes had told the story he now refused to tell.

She couldn't help it, her heart was wounded by his

silence and she wanted to press him in return. "Why haven't you ever married, Shakir? I'm sure there were lots of women who would've been thrilled at the prospect."

"There were a few women over the years."

"But none that interested you enough for marriage? That's strange. You asked me, why not one of them?"

He shrugged into his backpack and glanced up at the window, ignoring her. "Because none of them *were* you."

Chapter 9

Pure shock captured Nikki in a moment of deep regret. She'd asked for that remark, but now she wished she'd kept her mouth closed. How stupid of her to force the issue.

She'd known—should've known—how badly she had hurt him by sending him away all those years ago. But somehow she'd thought that if she didn't ever have to face the truth, it couldn't wound her in return.

She. Had. Hurt. Him. Seeing that was killing her, but it was a pain she would have to live with from now on. After all, he had hurt her, too.

Staring at Shakir as he ducked around the room, in and out of the cabin's shadows, her heart ached for the young man he'd been at twenty-four. She remembered feeling sure at the time that obeying her father's wishes was the best thing for everyone. How wrong she had been. How wrong they all were.

She'd grown up fast. Her childhood lie of a life had dashed before her very eyes. She'd gone from being a naïve and dutiful daughter to a cynical and practical single mother in a blink. When her supposed *intended* laughed at the idea of marriage to a pregnant pretender to the throne, her parents turned their backs on her plight.

She should have been smart enough to predict that outcome, but she'd been raised to trust. Trust in both her parents and the other advisors surrounding them to know what was best. That trusting nature had unfortunately remained with her, even after her father's downfall and death. She'd been so naïvely trusting that she'd lost her son to a complete stranger.

Now she trusted no one. Not even Shakir. Perhaps especially Shakir.

Nikki wondered again where he had disappeared to after she'd sent him away. He hadn't fought for her, and when she'd found out she needed him, he was gone. All these years later the memory of searching for him to no avail still haunted her and made her bitter. Why would a man who was about to graduate from university suddenly vanish like a puff of smoke into the night? To this day she could never completely trust him again.

She didn't dare ask him about it now. Asking would certainly lead to his inquiring why she'd bothered to come looking for him after declaring she never wanted to see him again. Her questions would wait for another time.

"What…" Her voice sounded rusty, hesitant. Just like she felt. "What are you doing?"

"I'm searching for a couple of decent bridles for us to use. Ones that might hold up for our trip."

She peered into the musty darkness. "I don't see any saddles in storage. Where do you suppose they keep them?"

Out of the room's farthest, darkest corner, he said, "It doesn't matter. We can't take the time to saddle the horses."

"Bareback? I've never been on a horse and you want me to ride bareback?" Her past temporarily forgotten with the intensity of her immediate future, she planted her hands on her hips. "I can't believe I let you talk me into this. We could've been hours closer to William now by walking."

"Nikki..." He sounded hard but hollow, as though he were slowly becoming a shell of himself.

She hadn't meant to imply that she'd disliked the way they'd spent their rest period. She had liked it, even though it was wrong of her to forget her mission, her baby, for even a moment. But it was his sullen attitude now that irritated her and made her angry.

"Don't 'Nikki' me. I want to lea—" The rest of her words were lost to a total blackout as the light coming in through the window was suddenly extinguished.

"Shh." Shakir's voice came out of the darkness. "Let your eyes get used to the light."

What light? Hugging herself around the middle, she froze, peering into nothingness.

In a blink she felt him right beside her. "You're about to get your wish. The soldiers are gone. We're leaving. Are you ready?"

He didn't give her a chance to answer, because before she knew what he intended, they were standing outside in the dry, fresh air. She was surprised at how well she could see in the light of the nearly full moon.

Shakir handed her a couple of small horse blankets then took her by the hand as they eased around the side of the storage building, heading for the paddock. She glanced in every direction, but they seemed to be alone, with only horses for company.

When they reached the fence, he stopped to whisper instructions in her ear. "I don't want to spook the animals. Too much noise and one of the soldiers might come out to check. Stand by the gate and try to make yourself seem small."

Nikki didn't want to "spook" the horses, either. Their dark outlines loomed like huge spectres against the night sky. She stood stock-still and tried shallow breathing.

Shakir bent between two fence rails and entered the paddock without so much as a rustle. He moved among the mighty steeds as if he was one of them. She could hear him murmuring something, but he was too far away for her to catch the words.

Sweat broke out on her upper lip. Her mouth turned to cotton. How would she ever manage to get on the back of one of these giants—let alone stay on?

Soon Shakir was by her side with two horses in tow. Too late to worry now. She must do this for her son. She bit down on the inside of her cheek and waited for him to show her what to do.

Taking the blankets, he threw one over the back of the largest horse and folded the other into his pack. "I'll give you a boost up. Hang on to the horse's mane until I join you."

"What?"

While she waited in vain for an answer, Shakir lifted

her, easing her bottom onto the blanket on the back of the bigger horse. Oh, great. She got the *big* one. The other horse looked much smaller from this angle. Maybe she could've handled that one.

Shakir helped gather her skirt under her and around her legs. She expected him to mount the other horse. But before she could even catch her breath, he threw a leg up and over the same horse where she was already seated and then slid behind her on the animal's back. Shakir slipped his wide arms around her waist and she noticed one of his hands held a long rope tied to the other horse.

"Balance lightly," he said softly. "Keep your legs relaxed and your back straight. That will help steady you."

How could she feel steady with him sitting this close? She could sense his heat. His warm breath on the back of her neck. His heartbeat pulsing through her back.

But the raging guilt about what they'd done ate at her gut. Kept her from sinking into all that temptation. She was a mother first. Not a woman with needs and desires. How could she have succumbed to that old devil lust while her baby was still in trouble?

"Stay quiet until we're off the mesa. Your lessons will come later."

Fine by her. She leaned back and let his body surround her. Protect her. For a while. For now.

As they slowly paraded into the wild night, Nikki couldn't help but think again of what they'd done together tonight. How physically close and intimate they'd become.

She wondered what it would be like if she'd married Shakir all those years ago. They would be a family now.

William would have a father to protect him and she and her child wouldn't be in danger.

Suddenly wishing she could talk to Shakir about her growing fears for her—their—son's safety, she decided she didn't like keeping the truth from him. Besides, the minute he saw William, Shakir would probably guess he was the boy's father. They looked so much alike. And what would William have to say? He had never asked about a father. Would he adjust?

Closing her eyes, she thought about telling both the men in her life the truth about each other. In her mind, she made it into a pretty picture. With everyone happy and smiling and eager to start a new life.

As the horse rocked gently under her, and Shakir cocooned her in his warm embrace, Nikki dreamed about someone else's life. A happy life, filled with her illusive ideal of love and family.

As dawn broke in a rainbow of pastels over the mountain peaks, Shakir looked toward Nikki sitting astride the second Taj pony. After all her worry and fear, he had never seen a woman take so quickly to riding bareback.

The rapid learning had probably come courtesy of her fierce determination to reach her son. As the miles went by, he'd sensed an angry energy building in the woman he loved. Her features were tight and there was an edge of violence in the way she held her shoulders.

She was different from who she'd been as a girl of nineteen when they'd first fallen in love. Not better or worse, but different. It was more than her changeover to motherhood. Many of the things he had once loved about her were still in evidence. She still had that aura of destiny about her. The beauty. The softness and the attitude of duty to others.

And…unfortunately for him, the overpowering sensual pull that made his heart slam into his rib cage every time she looked his way.

He should not have taken advantage of her back there in that primitive storage building with the enemy working only yards away from their heads. But when she'd kissed him and he'd touched her velvet skin, he'd fallen into such wild abandon that nothing mattered but the exhilaration of the two of them moving in tune—as one glorious being.

What he'd encountered was a bigger connection than just *something remembered*. This instinctual feeling was much more basic. His mouth had gone dry. His skin had burned. His mind had gone blank. He'd lost every bit of his good sense and took possession of her like a savage.

That could not ever happen again. She was too good and too urbane. He was—too violent and untamed. His best course of action from now on would be to use the connection between them to help her save her son. Then he would do the best thing for everyone—and let her go.

But from that day forward, he would keep watch over her from a distance. Never again would she be forced into a menial job and find herself taking chances with strangers to care for her child. He would devote his own life, and whatever fortune he'd accumulated, to affording her the kind of life she deserved. From a distance.

Somewhere in her future, Nikki would save people. Even if she couldn't be a royal, he foresaw her life as a leader and a public servant the way she'd been trained.

Shakir had no place in that destiny.

A ray of sunlight shot between two peaks and glowed across her face. That creamy skin of hers would burn too easily. Already her nose and cheeks were pink with the blush of sun.

He pulled their horses up in the shade of a basalt ledge. "We need a rest break here."

Frowning, she narrowed her eyes and tightened her lips. "Why? I'm all right. Let's keep moving."

Shakir dismounted and dropped the reins, allowing his horse to feed on tuffs of grass. "The horses need rest and water. They're bred for endurance, but one must never forget their needs, too. They've saved us a full day. We're only a few hours away from Kuh now."

"The horses. Of course. I hadn't thought of them." She slid off her mount and her knees promptly buckled under her.

He grinned like a drunken sod as he reached down to help her up. "You've been riding for a long time. It takes a while to get your ground legs back."

"I'll be fine. Just give me a moment."

Keeping his lips sealed, he held her close as she kicked out the kinks in her legs. The scent of her filled his nostrils. He would never forget it, or how she made him feel. His life was dedicated to her memory from now on.

"When you can stand alone, please drink some water and eat," he pleaded. "We still have a few packs of food that the Bedouin women made for us."

Nikki wrinkled up her nose but nodded her agreement. "I'm okay now. I'll drink as I walk around a little." She pulled away from him, took the canteen and marched down the canyon, backtracking the way they'd come.

He swung around to give water to the horses but spoke to her as he worked. "Don't go too far. You need to apply that SPF cream from the first aid kit since the sun is up."

She turned back but had to shield her eyes from the rising sun to look at him. "Yes, sir."

"Look, I know it's hard for you to accept help. But the only way you have any possibility of saving your son is for you to arrive safely. No falls. No infections. And no sunburns."

"What do you mean about it being hard for me to take help? I can accept help as well as anyone."

Shakir reached into his pack for the kit. "Uh-huh." Handing her the SPF cream, he gave her one of his best grins.

She sniffed but took the cream all the same.

"I'm going to call Tarik while the horses rest. We're close enough now and he should've had time to devise a plan."

Nikki didn't respond, but went to sit on a flat rock shelf in the shade as she applied cream to her face.

In minutes, Shakir had reached his brother on the solar-powered satellite phone. "What have you found?"

Tarik inhaled. "Trouble. You remember that there was an old iron ore plant in Kuh Friez?"

"Yes. Built originally by the Kasht but abandoned by the Taj years ago. When I was living with the Bedouin, the male teens used the old facility for war games. What about it?"

"Something's going on there. The town is busting

with people and commerce all of a sudden." Tarik cleared his throat. "I pulled a few strings with my former bosses at the American Department of Defense, and they checked the area out via satellite. It appears the Taj are excavating under that old site. In fact, they're doing a lot of heavy digging in the whole area."

"What for?"

"I've shown the satellite photos around and the consensus is it looks like the beginnings of an underground nuclear centrifuge facility. The scientists were surprised."

Nuclear? "Impossible. The Taj don't have that kind of scientific expertise."

"Enough money can buy almost anything, brother. And the Taj now have more than enough money."

For the first time since Shakir had entered Zabbarán, he experienced a moment of self-doubt. "Have you located the whereabouts of Nikki's son? Do we know where they're keeping him? And can we reach him there?"

"Prepare for more bad news, Shakir. The Taj elder Umar has been kidnapping young boys the same way he was kidnapping women. We know of at least six missing kids, all boys, but no one seems to know what he wants with them. Umar's sister and her husband are keeping the children in an abandoned house right on the grounds of the old plant."

Tarik paused, giving Shakir time to absorb the information. "I don't have to tell you that security is tight around that plant right now."

"But you do have a plan. A way in?"

"That depends. Do you remember the layout of the plant? Can you still find your way inside the fences?"

"I'm sure I can. What do you have in mind?"

"If you trust her to keep her head, you and Nikki will have a much better chance of sneaking inside the fences than would an entire squad. And the children won't fuss as much if a woman comes to their rescue. I'm sure they're all traumatized by now."

It took Shakir a second before he saw his brother's intentions. "Are you thinking you want to try for a rescue of all the children?"

"We must, brother." Tarik's determination oozed through the phone and reached Shakir's ear. "There really is no choice. We cannot leave them. It would be barbaric. But I would also like to give their captives a little surprise on the way out. Are you willing to help me?" Tarik added.

"I can't speak for Nikki, but I will do whatever is necessary." Shakir just had one small nonnegotiable demand. "As long as Nikki and her son make it out of Zabbarán none the worse for whatever you have in mind. If you can't guarantee that, then it's no-go."

"Listen to the plan and then talk to her. Let her decide."

Shakir agreed to listen and to put the question to Nikki, but he already knew the result. She would do anything, agree to anything, in order to reach her son. And the kind of person he knew her to be would never think of leaving behind other people's children. It simply wasn't in her DNA.

"What can you see?" Standing on a high, barren ridge, Nikki couldn't make out much in the dusty valley below.

Shakir let the binoculars drop and handed them to her. "Lots of action. See for yourself."

She held her breath and put the lens to her eyes. She wanted to see children—her child, but she knew it was too far away and the children would probably not be out in the hot afternoon sun anyway.

What came into her view was a town straight out of an American Western. Clapboard houses, tents set up to act as retail establishments, boards laid over sand and used as temporary sidewalks. If she hadn't known where they were, she would've guessed this place to be a movie set of a gold rush town.

Until—she spied Taj soldiers with assault rifles on every street corner. And jeeps filled with uniformed men with machine guns patrolling the perimeter fences of the ancient looking iron ore plant.

The plant itself had long ago been built in levels up against the side of mountain. A rusted hulk of metal and conveyor belts, it looked out of place located right next to a few newer concrète block buildings. Modern glass and stainless steel, the squat structures seemed to be office buildings. Or perhaps research facilities of some sort.

Their construction made them blend in with the cliffs behind them. Looking at them from this angle made her wonder if they could be spotted from above. Probably not.

Shakir had told her about the plant being converted over to something high tech. If he knew what kind of high tech business was going on there, he'd been careful not to mention it. Which gave her a bad case of nerves.

It was hard enough when he'd told her about Umar

kidnapping half a dozen boys along with William. The mental pictures of what her son had been going through became nearly unbearable now. But if she knew for certain what kind of terrible experiments the Taj were conducting at that plant, she was sure it would be far worse.

Shakir touched her arm. "Do you see the old plant manager's house on the grounds?"

She twisted to the right and caught sight of an ancient mud-brick, single-story building. "The children are being kept there?" It looked spooky and deserted.

"That's what our intel says."

"But why? What do they need with little kids?"

"You don't want to know that. Keep concentrating on setting them free and getting your son back."

She swallowed hard and nodded her head in agreement with him. His voice was quietly reassuring. It had always seemed to her that Shakir had an inner strength. Nothing rattled him.

But she was already so rattled that she could barely hold it together. She couldn't help it. They were close, and in a few hours she might have William back.

Dark despair crawled into her mind. But she couldn't let herself have any doubts. Shakir would definitely help her retrieve her son. By next week her baby would once again be home, sleeping with his stuffed bear in his own bed.

Nikki brushed away a tear. "How do we reach them?"

"There's a series of abandoned mine shafts in the cliffs behind the plant. They were boarded up and forgotten long ago. But one of them has a second entrance on the other side of that ridge. It comes out under the fence line and beside that old chute next to the house."

"Are you sure that shaft is still clear? Can we make it all the way to William?"

Shakir took her hands in his. "We *will* make it, Nik. We haven't come this far only to fail."

Chapter 10

Black as pitch, the mine shaft was steeper than Shakir remembered. He'd been negotiating the cavern and the old rail tracks fairly well using his NVGs, but having Nikki following in his footsteps with a small torchlight was becoming problematic. Every few feet she stumbled over a rock or fallen timber.

He'd needed her to accompany him on this mission. For rescuing the children if for nothing else. But the closer they came to the surface, to hostile territory, the more he wasn't certain she would be safe. Had he made a mistake by agreeing to bring her along?

As they slowly moved ahead, not speaking unless necessary, he occasionally heard rustling above their heads. Most likely, the sound was coming from a colony of desert bats. If other mammals could live in the environment, it was a good sign. At least this shaft hadn't filled with poisonous gases over the years.

But he was glad Nikki didn't know about the bats. She had enough on her mind.

The slight tingling he'd felt under his boots every now and then disturbed him more. His gut kept warning him that those quakes had to be the rumble of heavy machinery digging deep within the mountainside.

He was glad Nikki didn't know about that possibility, either. It concerned him because of the potential for structural damage that too much digging had on old mine shafts. He and Nikki certainly didn't need this tunnel falling in on their heads before they reached the Taj facility.

"Ow." Nikki's whispered yelp made him turn back to reach for her.

She was on her knees with the heavy skirt material twisted around her legs like a lasso. Looking more like a goose trussed up for roasting than the gorgeous blonde he respected and loved, Nikki was helpless inside her dress. Something had to give.

He hunkered down beside her. "Are you hurt? Cut?"

Shaking her head, she rubbed a hand across her face. "It's my ankle. I think it's only twisted, not sprained. But it hurts like the devil."

"Bedouin dresses aren't made for this sort of mission," he told her. "When we reach the end, we can do something about your clothing. But for now, I think I'd better carry you the rest of the way."

"Is that safe? What if you stumble in the dark?"

He grinned, knowing she couldn't see him with the low lighting. "Carrying you on my shoulders will be a lot safer than letting you stumble around. Remember how we did the carry before?"

She sighed. "Unfortunately, yes. I didn't like it, but it made the miles go faster."

Lifting her, he eased her up to his shoulders and draped her around his neck like a shawl. "Try to relax. I can balance better that way."

Her head was facing his chest, but she mumbled anyway. "Relax. Sure."

In a few moments, though, he noted most of her muscles going slack and her breathing slowed. He was proud of her efforts to be part of a team. She was one tough and determined woman.

After an hour of climbing, he turned a bend in the shaft and suddenly a soft rose-and-gold light shone straight ahead. Sunset. They'd reached the other end of the tunnel faster than he'd thought possible.

Shakir slowly lowered Nikki to her feet, but he kept her leaning against him until she got her bearings. "It looks like someone long ago fenced in the tunnel opening and salt bush has grown up along the fence. No problem for us, but I think we'd better wait until after sunset before we break through. Agreed?"

"Yes." She took in huge gulps of air and rubbed her arms and legs. "What can I do about all this dress material?"

"I can cut the bottom yardage off. But that will leave your legs bear. You can't be seen in public with no covering on your legs."

She leaned back and glared up at him. "If I'm seen in public here at all, I'm a dead woman. What does it matter what I'm wearing?"

He nodded, knowing how much more difficult this journey had been for her wearing those skirts. "Maybe we'll figure out something else once we're inside the plant facilities."

Setting to work with his hands, Shakir tore the material straight up a seam and then used the Ka-Bar to cut a horizontal line right above her knees. The edge wasn't exactly straight and the dress not quite a miniskirt, but the length would be every bit as shocking to the backward civilization in Zabbarán. For his part, well, he thought she had a terrific pair of legs and was pleased to see them again.

"The sleeves, too, please. They're hot." She held out her arms and waited.

"Long sleeves are important in the desert sun."

"I won't still be here at tomorrow's sunrise. Will I?" She looked so hopeful, so trusting all of a sudden, that he couldn't deny her request.

"All right. But just in case, let's compromise at right above the elbow. Okay?"

She nodded and he complied, carefully cutting the material while avoiding her skin. "Now what?" she asked as she looked toward the daylight.

"Now we wait until dark." He moved to the tunnel entrance and settled down on the rocky ground.

"I can't sit still. I have to move while we wait. Maybe I can walk out the pain in my ankle."

"Whatever you like." Shakir wasn't sure he could stand to have her sitting beside him or resting against him in any case.

The temptation to take her, any way he could get her, was far too great. No, he would be wise to remember his vow to watch out for her from a distance.

Starting right now.

* * *

Baghel, the captain of the Taj guards, rode into Kuh Friez along with two squads of men just as the sun was setting behind purple mountain peaks. Irritation rode with him in the horse's saddle. Irritation, along with a growing, insidious fear.

His commission in Umar's guard, perhaps his very life, depended upon his ability to safeguard all of the elder's projects. That meant Baghel was responsible for security here in Kuh Frieze along with all his other duties. But the women prisoners in the fortress had already been stolen from Umar, and Baghel's instincts were telling him that the plan to keep children imprisoned in Kuh and also the elder's secret building venture were both in imminent danger.

Dismounting, he strode into the lone two-story security building at the project's edge. A foreigner with a business suit met him at the front desk.

"You must be Captain Baghel of Umar's guards," the foreigner said with a smarmy smile. "I'm Anatolii Chapaev. I'm in charge here." The man stuck his bare hand out.

Baghel stared down at the offending appendage and fought his first inclination. Chopping off useless and insolent hands or heads was a big part of Taj Zabbar heritage. His ancestors had thought it necessary to take swift action when dealing with inferiors. But in this case, the captain refrained from doing what came naturally in order to learn more.

He stood at parade rest and folded his hands behind his back. "In charge of what, Mister Foreigner?"

The man withdrew his arm and scowled. "The special project your government is undertaking at this old iron ore facility. I am the project manager. What can I do for you?"

Without answering, Baghel looked around, then swiftly backhanded the asinine foreigner across his face. The man's knees buckled. Silent, the foolish man put a palm to his rosy cheek and stared dumbfounded.

"You can do nothing for the Captain of Umar's guards, fool. I am here to take charge of all security surrounding this *special* project."

"But…" The man looked hesitant to speak, but finally straightened and dared to put voice to his words. "We already have security. Soldiers like yourself. The council of elders assured us that…"

"Be quiet. I saw no soldiers on the road into town. No guards at the gate. Even the house of the Royal Princess, Umar's sister, is not outwardly guarded. Where are the weapons to stop intruders? Where are the towers to keep watch of the prisoners?"

A quick frisson of amusement passed through the foreigner's eyes. It was all the captain could do not to draw his sword and cut the man down where he stood. There was nothing amusing about the situation that Baghel could see.

"In the first place," the stranger began with feigned patience. "The prisoners, as you call them, are mere children. I can't imagine why you are holding…" The foreigner stopped himself and looked contrite. "It's none of my business. But I don't think you have anything to fear on the babies' account.

"In the second place," the fool continued. "The Taj Zabbar council of elders wants to keep our entire undertaking away from prying eyes. They don't want the world to know what we're doing here at Kuh Frieze."

The foreigner looked smug and kept talking. "It's a secret project. Furthermore, we have our own methods of security. High tech surveillance equipment. We knew you and your men were heading into town an hour before you arrived. And without having to sacrifice any manpower to do it."

The captain waved the man's objections away. "Cameras? Nonsense. What good are cameras? If an assault is made, you need men and you need weapons. Not cameras."

"An assault? But that's ridiculous. The only real potential for assault would come from the air. And we have radar surveillance. We will know of any air attacks ahead of time. Your air force will knock whoever or whatever it is out of the sky."

Captain Baghel unholstered his pistol and pointed it directly at the man's forehead. "I am in charge of security for all the elder Umar's projects. I say what will happen."

"Yes. Of course."

"Good. And I say we need more men with weapons to protect the projects in Kuh Frieze. I will place trained men at strategic points around the fence's perimeter and in various spots on the facility grounds."

"But then it won't remain a secret. I don't think…"

Baghel cocked the trigger. The foreigner lifted his hands, palms out, as sweat began to trickle down his neck.

Going on as though he had not been rudely interrupted, Baghel added, "I believe it would be smart to move the children out of that indefensible house. I want them put in a safer place where we can make sure they cannot be reached."

"Where? We have no prisons. That's not our job."

"Are there finished rooms under the earth?"

The foreigner nodded. "Yes, several layers are complete, though..." He looked ready to make another objection, but thought better of it.

"It is settled." The captain replaced his weapon. "We move the children tonight." He turned and started for the door.

Before opening the door, Baghel turned back. "I have been notified that at least two foreigners are headed on foot through the desert to Kuh Frieze. I intend to find them. Stop them. And execute them."

"But why are they coming here? Who are they?"

"Enemies of the Taj," the captain told him lightly. "It doesn't matter why. All foreigners are enemies of the Taj."

He glared at the *foreign* project manager. "You would be well advised to do as I command. If you or your men see these two foreigners before they are found by my soldiers, notify me at once."

Shakir was almost finished cutting through the rusty wire fence at the tunnel's entrance when the satellite phone vibrated at his side. He stopped to answer his brother's call.

"We've located the shaft's eastern entrance right where you said it would be. Six men are starting in your direction," Tarik said through the earpiece. "How close are you?"

"Nikki and I are already at the facility end. And I'm almost through the fence barrier covering this entrance. The tunnel is wide open all the way."

"Good." Tarik's voice was loud and clear. "We're

staging the helicopters in that blind canyon on the side of the mountain that you mentioned. It was a tricky approach and landing, but I'm sure the Taj radar didn't catch any sign of us."

Tarik went on, "We're close enough now to your position that you should be able to begin wearing the earbud and mouthpiece. All is ready for the operation on our end. But..." Tarik hesitated and the idea of his younger brother being unsure bothered Shakir. Still, he said nothing and waited.

"There's been a change," Tarik finally said. "One of our covert agents in Kuh Frieze reports the children are being moved out of the house as we speak."

"Moved? Moved to where?"

"Hard to tell. But they haven't been brought out through the gates. My guess is the Taj are relocating them to the interior of the plant facility in order to better protect them. All of a sudden this facility, the whole town, is swamped with Taj soldiers. They're patrolling the streets and the plant's fence line. I would tell you to be careful," Tarik added. "But I know you will anyway."

"Thanks," Shakir grumbled as he tried to process the new information.

"By the way, brother, these extra soldiers all seem to be coming from the cavalry. Probably under Captain Baghel's command. You realize that means they won't be outfitted with any modern weapons or warfare equipment, don't you?"

Shakir smiled into the dark. "Yes. Baghel is an old enemy. We know his style."

And Shakir couldn't wait to outwit his nemesis and retrieve Nikki's son. The time had come to make a move.

Not for the first time, Nikki wished she had spent more time learning the Taj Zabbar language before she'd flown to Zabbarán to find her son. She and Shakir were squatting below the window of a tiny guard shack right inside the fence, eavesdropping on one side of a soldier's phone conversation.

Though the moon was full and she could see fairly well, Shakir had assured her that her dark clothing would keep the soldiers from spotting them in the shadows. Straightening the black scarf on her head that covered her blond hair and trying to shrink down into the shorter dress length, she sure hoped he was right.

Shakir told her the children were being moved, and that the two of them needed to be careful not to run into the soldiers who'd been stationed around the plant's fence line. But now they would have to search for the children throughout the whole facility. How were they going to avoid being spotted?

The soldier inside the shack quit speaking and she could hear him moving around the room. Within a few moments, the light went out and door on the other side of the building opened and then quickly shut again.

Shakir leaned close. "The guard has been ordered to a perimeter position. This is our chance."

Chance for what? she wondered. When Shakir motioned for her to follow, she moved directly behind him and stuck to him like a second set of clothes.

But when he inched around the guard shack, opened

the door, crawled inside and ushered her in, too, she was shocked. What was he thinking?

Leaving the light turned off, Shakir quietly closed the door behind them. "Listen for anyone coming. I'm going to look for plans to the new facility. It's a long shot that they'd keep a set of plans in a guard shack but it's a chance worth taking."

Nikki blew out a breath of air and leaned her back against the door. They were in the belly of the beast, and she wondered if Shakir could really protect them as well as he imagined. She agreed that he was certainly good at survival tactics; he'd brought them here after all. But could he take on an entire squad of Taj soldiers?

As Shakir rifled through papers and file drawers, Nikki's mind rifled through thoughts just as fast. If they were destined to die in this place, she wanted to make sure her son was okay first. Beyond that, she needed enough time to tell Shakir the truth.

She would hate it if he died before knowing he was a father. Confused and afraid of what he made her feel, of what would happen to her and William if he turned away, Nikki tried to be honest—at least with herself.

Her whole life had been a series of disappointments. She'd learned the hard way not to count on anything but her own efforts. At this point she was afraid to pin her hopes on loving Shakir. He had already disappointed her more than once.

And she didn't want to raise her son's hopes, either. She was doing her best to teach William not to count on anyone else. It would only hurt him in the end.

William. What was best for him? What was he doing right now?

Fisting her hands, she worked hard trying not to

think too much about her son. They were almost there. She could already feel her arms around him. No sense working herself up too soon. William would need her to be on her toes. And ready for anything.

"Nothing here." Shakir crawled back to where she was sitting, taking care not to move past the front window. "No maps or drawings. No computer. Nothing."

He sat beside her. "I'll have to make a recon tour around the facility. But I want you to stay here."

"Here? In the guard shack? Uh-uh. I want to go with you."

Shakir took her hand. "I can't be worried about you while I'm scouting. Stay here—in the shadows behind the shack. You'll be safe and I'll be back before you know I was gone."

Ripping her hand from his, she glowered at him through streaks of moonlight. "Do I have a choice?"

"That's my girl."

Nikki nearly growled her disapproval of the term, but figured it would be a waste of time. "Fine. Let's go."

They crept back into the night air and waddled on their haunches to the back of the shack. Nothing but empty fencing behind the shack. Shakir was right. She should be safe enough to wait here.

"Come back soon—or come back with my son." She tried to make Shakir hear her pleas through the tone of her voice.

"You will have your son tonight. And I will return soon with a better plan. Wait."

Nikki settled down with her back to the shack's wall. But looking out to nothing but mountain desert landscape made her more frightened than ever. She closed her eyes and wrapped her arms around her knees.

With her eyes closed, thoughts of William sprang into her head again. Where was her baby? Was he okay?

She thought back to the day she'd given birth. To how frightened she'd been for William on that day, too. All alone, she had taken a bus to the hospital in Paris. Worried about her baby's health, she'd fought through twenty hours of labor all by herself. Then when William was born in good health, she worried about how they would survive.

Luckily, her father had relented and brought his daughter and grandson home. It didn't make them part of a happy family unit, but it kept them alive. When her father died, probably of a broken spirit after losing his bid to return to the throne, Nikki had once again thought about contacting Shakir. This time for purely selfish reasons. She'd needed help.

But a cursory check on his whereabouts gained her nothing. It was as if he'd disappeared directly into the atmosphere like a ghost. She'd even started to believe she had imagined their whole relationship. That there was no real person named Shakir Kadir.

Suddenly the hair on Nikki's arms stood straight up. Someone was coming. Shakir?

Opening her eyes and adjusting them to the darkness, she turned her head in time to see the outline of a man as he turned the corner of the shack. But what was that he was carrying? His assault rifle?

Once the figure was fully around the edge of the building, Nikki saw the true picture. It was not an assault rifle, and it was not Shakir.

This was a much shorter Taj soldier and he was carrying a rifle fitted with a bayonet. A bayonet?

Nikki jumped to her feet as the soldier spotted her

and pointed his rifle directly at her chest. The man sputtered words in the Taj language, but Nikki clearly understood what he was trying to say.

She raised her hands in the air. But that didn't seem to satisfy the soldier. He rammed his bayonet in her direction, just missing her chest by inches.

Swinging the rifle, the soldier spoke angry words as he glared at her naked legs. She jumped, but the blade caught her on the thigh. Blood oozed from the wound and it was all she could do not to cry out.

But she didn't have time to scream. The soldier kept swinging and ramming his weapon at her legs. This man intended to keep cutting her until she either bled out or couldn't stand under her own power.

Did she dare try to run? Would he shoot? Where could she go?

Desperate, Nikki kept backing up, darting left and right and trying to avoid the blade. Tears sprang from her eyes as she pleaded with the soldier to stop.

As Nikki watched the man's face for any slip up in his concentration or any sign of compassion, she saw a dark shadow looming behind his back. Another soldier? She imagined much worse trouble would befall her if more soldiers arrived to torment and torture.

Before she could react, the gigantic shadow stepped close and captured the soldier in a tight-fisted embrace. Through the moonlight, she saw the flash of a blade as it slashed across the man's throat.

Instantly, silently, it was all over. Blood came spurting from the neck wound. A wound that had ended the man's life.

The soldier's body crumpled to the ground. And when

she looked up, Shakir was coming toward her. His face a mask. This was not a man she recognized.

Nausea hit her hard as the adrenaline flowed through her like warm wine. Her body began to shake. She doubled over and put her head down but it was too late. She felt herself falling into a deep, dark well of oblivion.

Chapter 11

"You came back." Nikki trembled in Shakir's arms and shivered against his neck. "You really came."

"I said I would return."

When he'd seen her crumpling to the ground, his veins had burned with fear for her. He hadn't taken a breath until she'd come to from her faint. She wasn't out cold for long, but he found his own hands trembling while waiting for her to come around.

Spotting blood on her dress, he held back the rage that sprang up in his gut. "Are you injured?"

"A small cut is all. But I thought I was going to die. Thank God you came in time and saved me." She clung to his neck and tried to regulate her breathing. He felt her heart beat wildly as she pressed against his chest.

He hated that she'd had to face death again like that. If he'd arrived a few minutes later—

Even worse than almost losing her, he couldn't stand that she'd seen his true nature. Violence was a big part of who he was. A part he'd kept hidden for the time they'd been together, and that he wished he could've kept her from knowing even now.

But a man could not change who he was inside. And Shakir was a killer. He'd first taken the life of a man at the age of fifteen. Tribal warfare, savage and real, was where he'd lost his childhood. His weapon of choice then had been a knife. But using a knife meant he'd had to get close—and personal. Close enough to see the man's eyes and feel his life force draining from his body.

From then on, his own life had become one long horror-filled show of mutilated bodies and pools of blood, staying with people no better than the Taj Zabbar. In a world far different from the Kadir family tradition of congenial trade where he'd spent his early years. But his mother's father had insisted he survive and live where he could not avoid the savagery. In order to make him into a warrior. A male adult member of the tribe.

"I didn't believe you would really show up in time," Nikki cried. "You didn't bef…no one ever…" She buried her head in his shoulder and couldn't continue.

But he got the message. Someone, probably William's father, had left her in the lurch. As hysterical as she was, perhaps many people had walked away rather than help her out. Her parents. The Paris police. Who else?

So that must be the reason why it seemed hard for her to ask for help. When hope was kicked from a person for enough times, they gave up. The darkness rose inside him again. He wanted to murder all the people in her life who had abused her so.

But he was helpless to fix the past. All he could do

was be there for her now. To help her save her son and bring them both back to civilization. Then, when they were truly safe and out of all danger, he would save her from his own brand of violence, too.

She deserved happiness. A peaceful existence. He would see that she got that—without the perilous atmosphere that always surrounded his life.

He'd tried to save her once before from everything that was dark inside him. He'd walked away rather than fight for her because he hadn't wanted to impose his rash nature on her finer sensibilities. She'd had a chance to be what she was destined to become. Or at least, he'd thought she was being offered that chance. But he'd been wrong not to stick around behind the scenes and watch out that she didn't get hurt. He saw that now.

But at the time—at the time—

Nikki stirred in his arms. "William? Did you find the children?"

"Not yet. I didn't locate any plans of the facility, either. But I did notice a lot of soldiers guarding an old drainage pipe and slag tower. The one near the vent house and conveyor drain. Doesn't make any sense for soldiers to guard anything that's abandoned and useless. My guess is something important is hidden in there. Maybe in a storage bin or superstack."

"Oh, no. I can't stand thinking of my baby there. Or any of the other children. How are we going to reach them with all the soldiers around?"

"I have a plan. I've contacted Tarik and he agrees. But first we have to take care of a few things here."

She sat up and looked over at the body of the soldier. "Yes. We need to hide that." She waved her arm at the dead man as though he were trash to be swept away.

Shakir was stunned that she could treat death so casually. "I'll take care of the body. I don't want you to deal with it."

"I want to do my share," she implored. "Whatever is necessary to rescue my son and the other children. I hate that anyone would take babies from their parents for God knows what reason. Anyone who can do that is not human. They deserve whatever they get."

Surprised at her attitude, Shakir nevertheless had no time to discuss it. "I'll handle disposing of the body. Meanwhile, I located something else while I was scouting that you might like."

He pulled the garment from his pack. "I was hiding in the laundry, while trying to avoid a confrontation, and came up with these." Holding out the soldier's slacks, he grinned at her. "They're the smallest size I could find."

"A pair of pants? Wonderful. Let me have them."

"Wait." He handed her one of the antibiotic wipes. "Clean your leg wound first."

She nodded and set to work. While she tended her injury and slipped on the slacks, he hefted the body and carted it to the fence line. On the far side, several tamarisks and cabbage plants grew nearby. It would probably take a day or two for anyone to spot the body under there. With any luck, the scavengers would not venture this close to humans until the smell tempted them out in the open in a couple of days.

By then, he planned for all of them—Nikki, the children and Tarik's entire team—to be long gone.

Nikki had needed to tie the Bedouin woman's sash around the waistband of the soldier's pants like a belt and then had to roll the cuffs up three times to make them fit. But as she crawled along behind Shakir on the uphill side of the mountain right beyond the fence, she was grateful for the protection. And for the black material hiding her pale skin in the dark.

Shakir's plan seemed too tricky and slightly too dangerous. But on the other hand, his brother said the whole town was filling up fast with soldiers. It was the only plan they had.

After disposing of the body, Shakir had led her through a hole he'd popped in the fence while she was changing. She hadn't liked the idea of leaving the facility grounds without William, but Shakir said they wouldn't go far before they would be back on the other side of the fence.

She wasn't too sure at this point how that was ever going to happen. Already they'd had to stop and lay flat on the ground in order to avoid being caught by soldiers patrolling the fence. More and more soldiers seemed to be stationed along the facility's perimeter.

As they crawled over rocks and sand, her mind filled with inconsequential thoughts. Like how proud she felt that Shakir had thought enough of her abilities to bring her into the middle of the danger. She was becoming surer of her own abilities every day.

Not just a helpless ex-royal anymore, she was far from weak. She wondered when Shakir had first noticed the truth of what kind of woman she was underneath the soft and sweet feminine trappings.

Shakir. He was exactly the right man for this rescue. Why hadn't she seen his ruthless determination and fierce fighting spirit before? She'd always thought of him as a dashing sheik, a mysterious prince of the desert.

More movie star than real Bedouin warrior. Even when he'd come for her and dragged her out of the harem prison she hadn't really opened her eyes to the light. There was so much more to him than the prince of the desert image.

Perhaps this tough and rugged attitude of his had always been a part of him. Hidden deep like hers was. Underneath a shiny veneer. Or it could've been his attitude was that one special something she'd noticed in his eyes as a girl but couldn't name then. Or maybe she'd been too young that long ago to really understand.

How had she gotten so lucky to have him fall back into her life at just the right moment?

And how was she ever going to tell him the truth now? She would tell him. Soon. She'd even begun to relish the idea of seeing his expression when she told him that William was his son.

Surprise? No doubt.

Delight? One could only pray.

Hurt? She hoped not too badly and not for too long.

Disappointment? That idea brought her up short. She assumed she might see disappointment in his eyes when he realized all the years he had missed with his son. But she assured herself that he could not blame her. Not when she explained how desperately she'd searched for him to tell him he was going to be a father. He had missed the years, but not for the lack of her attempts to find him.

Maybe after her revelation, Shakir would reciprocate and tell her where he'd gone when he'd walked away all those years ago. Then there would be no secrets between them anymore.

The idea of the three of them, mother and father and son, living together as a family unit gave her a snug and cozy feeling all over. She let the warmth of that thought wind around inside her heart, bringing her an easy, calm mood.

Until…she looked up ahead and saw the hulking relic of the old iron ore plant.

Lopsided metal buildings, a super smokestack, conveyor belts and rusted metal pipes. The profusion of ancient iron works resembled a ghost city with its eerie spotlights shining against the ruins of a once prosperous facility. Somewhere off in the distance near the front gate, she knew there were a few newer buildings. But this old section seemed to be a puzzle of deteriorating evil spirits.

Shakir climbed higher up the side of the mountain, farther and farther away from the fence. She didn't want to go that way—in the opposite direction from her baby. But Shakir's plan called for this—so she let him lead.

Soon, she saw an enormous obstacle in their path. The drain and slag pipe he'd told her about that was built over the fence. But it looked gigantic in the dark. How would they ever use this rusted piece of slick, gray metal to enter the plant when it was too tall and too round to climb?

Shakir waited at the base for her to catch up. "There's a drain bridge on the other side of the pipe," he whispered. "But we have to go up and over to reach it."

She turned her head and glanced right and left, to be sure there weren't any major breaks in the pipe where they could just duck underneath instead. But there weren't any, not for as far as she could see. Besides,

Shakir had played on these premises as a boy. He would know if there was any other way.

"How?"

He pointed to the metal rivets and stitches on the pipe. "Those will have to do as a ladder. Take your shoes off."

He was the leader. She was the follower. Despite her misgivings, she crouched down beside him and removed her leather-soled sandals. Then Shakir tied the two of them together again at the waist as he had when they'd gone up the cliff near the horse barn.

But this pipe was a slicker surface. With far fewer footholds, and the ones they did have were narrow and shallow. Looking straight up to the top of the pipe, she couldn't even see that far in the dark. The giant drain pipe must be fifteen feet tall and probably at least that wide.

She was terrified. But when Shakir patted her shoulder and then began his assent, she followed in his footsteps. And tried not to look down or up.

Just as she was beginning to think of herself as a mountain goat, they reached the top and Shakir grabbed for her waist when her feet wanted to go out from under her. He deftly balanced the two of them on the rounded surface of the pipe while a hot desert breeze battered their bodies and whipped at their clothes.

"Now for the tricky part," he said quietly.

Now? What had they been doing up to this point?

"I'm going to lower you down to the bridge. Think you remember the lesson on rappelling?"

She nodded. If she didn't remember, she would make it up. Anything to climb off the metal pipe and go back to searching for her son on solid ground.

Down on her hands and knees, she closed her eyes and went over the side, hanging on to the scarf tied between them like her lifeline. But when her feet slipped off the metal and left her dangling in midair, it didn't even occur to her not to trust in Shakir to keep her safe. He would. All she had to do was reach—

Her feet suddenly touched the wooden surface of the bridge at about midpoint on the side of the pipe. When she gained her footing, Shakir scrambled down, too.

The old wood bridge was shaky and some of the boards were rotted out. But it was a far better solution than trying to balance on the top of the pipe. And much preferable to fighting their way inside past the guards with guns. They rushed to put on their shoes.

Once again, Shakir went ahead, testing each board before he stepped down. Nikki was getting good at following his lead.

When they reached the spot on the bridge that straddled the fence line, they hugged the side of the pipe and slid by like a couple of shadows. All the while hoping no one would look up and see them walking past. Shakir said he'd noticed cameras at various vantage points along the fence and on some of the buildings. But he assured her they were easy to avoid by staying in the darkness.

All she cared about was that they were back on facility property. Back to where the Taj were keeping William prisoner.

The drain bridge ended at a doorway to a large elevator shaft. A rickety, wood-slatted structure, it looked pretty wobbly to her. Shakir urged her to keep going. When he came to the door, though, he found it locked. That didn't slow him down for long.

He rammed his shoulder against the aging door and the lock gave. But when he stepped into the gloom ahead, a sudden shower of wood splinters shattered down around her head and shoulders.

Shakir grabbed her arm, pulled her inside and closed the door behind them. "That was a sniper's bullet. Someone evidently spotted us."

Someone was shooting at them? *Ohmygod.*

"Are you hurt?"

She brushed at the wood bits and pieces on her clothes. "I don't think so. What are we going to do?" Her voice was a stage whisper full of fright. She couldn't help it.

"We'll leave the sniper to Tarik." Shakir sounded calm and unruffled. "And you and I are going on to rescue your son."

Shakir stood still for a second and got his bearings in the pitch darkness. Finally he gave up and reached for the NVGs. The old elevator stack smelled of decay and the effects of the elements.

They were standing on a metal landing and beside them was a rung ladder stretching down into the nothingness below. He might've been disappointed at not finding any visible signs of construction, nor any evidence of the children, except for the hum of mechanical equipment pulsating through his feet. Somewhere close by, below them in the earth, machines were running. Machines operated by humans. Either construction workers or soldiers. There must be a way in from here.

"Do you feel that?" he asked Nikki.

"Sort of. What is it?" But then he saw her peering

down into the elevator shaft. "There's something down there. Tiny rays of light and something else I can't tell… We have to go down."

He agreed. This time, he intended to protect her with the full resources of his body. Starting below, he tested out the sturdiness of the ladder. It seemed solid enough. After taking the first ten steps down, he moved to the side and let her step onto the ladder, too.

His heart stilled as he hoped to hell the ladder would support them both. When it did and she was completely on the ladder, his heart started up again while he grabbed hold of the rungs above her head, covering her body with his own. If anyone shot at them now, he would be the one to take the hit.

It was difficult crabbing their way down the ladder in such a cautious fashion. And the closer to the bottom they came, the louder the hum of machines and the more the vibrations seemed to shake the entire shaft.

At odd moments, he felt as if the whole elevator building would come crashing down around their heads in a shower of split boards and sawdust. It took about twenty minutes of difficult descent but at last they came to another landing and another door that Shakir felt sure must be below ground level.

He shoved Nikki to safety on one side of the door, withdrew his semi-automatic and tried the knob. It wasn't locked. That made him bloody well nervous.

But they had no choice except to move on. They could not go backward. At this point that sniper may have already called in an alarm and a whole regiment could be waiting on the other side of the door for them to reappear.

Shakir put his back against the wall and used a

backhanded grip on the knob to open the door. The hinges squeaked a bit, but the door opened with little trouble. Sounds of machinery filled the musty air. He peeked inside and found a poorly lit room filled with equipment.

"What is this place?" Nikki asked in a raised voice to be heard over the din.

He could only guess. "I suspect they're using the elevator shaft for ventilation. And this is the air handling equipment. But this room's in another underground building. New construction with a concrete floor. There must be another entrance."

Taking her by the hand, he wound their way past the many air handlers and whirring fan motors. Some of the equipment looked large enough to power an entire city.

Under an eerily lit red sign written in the Russian language, he found the exit door. After another moment of extreme caution, he opened the door and they stepped out. They found themselves in a massive but empty hallway with low lighting and a long stretch of tile floor. It also looked like new construction.

But it felt too open. Too unprotected. He didn't like moving into a space that was so exposed. But then again, the choice was going forward or nothing.

He flipped off the NVGs and took a few steps. "Hug the wall and stay behind me," he told her.

They traveled a few yards but found no doorways or offshoot hallways. Continuing straight ahead, he finally spotted what looked like the doors to an interior elevator at the end of the hall.

Not good. At any moment those doors could slide open and they would be as good as dead.

Moving even more carefully now, they inched on, one step at a time.

Just before they reached the elevator doors, they came to an alcove and another short hallway off to a right angle of where they stood. Two or three closed doors were visible, leading off the smaller hall.

"What is that thing?" Nikki pulled her hand from his grip and started down the smaller, dimmer corridor.

"Nik, wait!" But her attention was riveted to something unknown on the floor, and she acted as if she didn't even hear him call.

This was a terrible time for her to go off on her own and lose focus. Shakir turned the corner, too, and hurried after her.

He took bigger steps and came up behind her fast. But as he stretched out his hand to take her by the shoulder, she bent over out of his reach as she picked the object up off the floor.

"Oh, dear God." Crumbling to her knees, she gasped and doubled over.

"What is it?" Shakir gently pulled her back to her feet and tried to see what she was holding.

She finally looked up at him, unshed tears welling in her eyes, and opened her hand. He couldn't see what the object was at first, but took it from her to study.

When at last he recognized the focus of her pain, his knees wobbled under him, too. For there in his palm lay a little boy's tiny toy soldier.

Chapter 12

"Is it his? William's?"

Nikki could barely breathe. "Yes. No. I don't know. It could be."

Even if it wasn't her son's toy, the mere sight of the tiny soldier had made her realize how real everything was. This was no war game they were playing. Real children were in danger. Her son. Other mothers' sons.

Why hadn't they brought along an entire army to back them up against such evil?

The sound of elevator doors sliding open captured her attention. She looked to Shakir to make sure she wasn't dreaming. He put his finger to his lips and backed them up to a doorway.

Before she could begin to worry, he wrapped an arm around her waist and ducked into whatever room lay behind the door. After letting her loose, he waited with his ear to the door and his gun in his hand. She stood still behind him, but glanced around to check the room where they'd taken refuge.

Not so much a room as it was a tiny lobby, they'd stepped into the maintenance hall where anyone could access both an elevator and a stairwell. She didn't like standing in front of another elevator doorway. But until Shakir gave the signal, she was afraid to move.

"They've walked past the alcove," he said in the low voice she was becoming accustomed to hearing. "Going to the air handler room, is my guess. I hope they're not searching for us."

When he turned and saw the maintenance elevator, he punched the call button before she could caution him against it. "We need to know how many floors we're dealing with."

The doors slid open in a moment and Shakir ducked his head inside to study the call button panel. "Ten floors." He jerked himself back out of the way of the closing doors without touching anything in the process. "We know we didn't climb down any ten floors in that wooden elevator shaft."

He flicked a glance at the stairwell, with stairs going both up and down. "Stand here and be quiet for one second." With that remark, he sprinted up the stairs.

She waited, but her legs were shaking so badly it was hard to stay quiet. Her teeth chattered with cold fear.

She didn't have to wait long. In a few minutes Shakir was back on her level.

"It's only one flight up. There must be eight floors below us. That's pretty deep into the mountain."

"Where are the children? Which floor?"

She could see him almost rolling his eyes at her inane question, but he held back. "No way to know until we try them all. I'm fairly sure they aren't on this level. You?"

"I agree. This floor seems to be mostly equipment. What did you see upstairs?"

"Another lobby. But that floor looks like the entrance to the whole works. From what I could tell, they've disguised the access to this building behind one of the old vent houses."

"So we go down." She turned and headed for the stairwell.

"Hold it." Shakir took her arm. "Let me go first, do the checking. I suspect my instincts have been more finely honed than yours."

She actually felt like smiling. "You don't know much about a mother's instincts, do you?"

"No. I don't. But I wish…" The sadness in his unfinished answer threw her off for a moment. "Never mind. I still need to go first."

Standing aside, she let him creep down the stairs in front of her without asking him to finish his thought. She held on to his belt buckle and tried not to trip as they descended as silently as possible.

When they peeked through the door on the next level down, Nikki was surprised to see a maze of hallways and doors. The floor wasn't built in the same configuration as the one above. Not at all.

"This looks like a possibility," Shakir told her. "But I want to see what's below us before we wander around these halls too much."

Nikki bounced on her toes, eager to search. But

as Shakir started down the stairs again, she kept up with him.

The next floor down was totally different again. This time the one giant space seemed to be under construction. Sawhorses, wallboards, pieces of tile strewn around, the rooms on this floor obviously were not finished. But she couldn't see any workmen. The place was deserted.

"Wait here." Once again Shakir raced down the stairs without her.

"There's nothing below us but more construction," he said when he was back by her side. "Levels one through six are inaccessible via this stairwell. I'd bet that's where they're building the centrifuge."

"That deep underground?"

Shakir inhaled deeply and blew out a breath. "All the better to keep it a secret from the world."

"These really are very bad people, aren't they?"

He didn't answer, but she knew.

"I need to contact Tarik, but I'm not sure I can reach him from this far underground." Shakir stood a moment and seemed to be debating a new plan. "Let's go back up to the floor under construction. I think I spied something there that could help us."

Shakir paused as they stepped through the doorway to the unfinished floor. At least he was sure they had the right floor narrowed down. The children had to be one flight up in one of the many rooms on that level. But which room? He and Nikki couldn't very well go up and down the halls brazenly checking every room.

It was a good bet that Captain Baghel already knew about the two foreigners on the facility grounds. But from this depth in the earth, Shakir could not talk to Tarik on their military style comm unit so he could find out for sure. He couldn't reach his brother by satellite phone, either. Not from here.

"What are we doing?" Nikki's voice held a combination of bravado and reckless agitation.

He knew she was growing more and more impatient to find her son. Shakir didn't blame her. But he couldn't allow her to become careless.

"We're taking the long way going up one level."

Her face became a puzzle of confusion and agitation. But she clamped her mouth shut as she followed him to the outer wall of the one big space. They clung to the unpainted wall while they crept farther into the room, but stayed well away from the center. If anyone happened upon them, they could take cover more easily this way.

When they closed in on the farthest corner, Shakir was pleased to see that he'd guessed right. A workman had walked away from the job, leaving the ceiling panels off and the air ducts wide open.

"Here we go." He looked up at the opening, judging how much space was available.

"You're nuts." She was staring up at the opening, too. "We can't go up there. *You* can't go. The ceiling won't hold you."

"Only one way to find out." It wasn't much of a jump for him to grab hold of the duct's framing and swing himself up. Another good swing of his legs and he was crouching inside the five-by-five aluminum sheet metal air duct.

"Seems to be holding fine. I guess the Taj aren't half

bad at fabricating metalworks. Everybody has to be good at something."

She didn't laugh. Not even a smile.

"Yeah, not too funny. Considering the circumstances." He rolled over until he was lying flat out on his stomach with his arms reaching down through the opening. "Catch hold of my arms. I'll lift you up."

Looking more than a little skeptical, she didn't hesitate for long before she did as he asked. He was impressed by her. She was a real soldier, following his command no matter what she must be thinking. He was beginning to admire everything about her. In addition to being gorgeous and sexy, tough and loving, she was also a survivor.

He already knew that he loved her. But this new awareness of her was something out of his experience. It was something for him to study and mull over—later.

Shakir grabbed her arms and pulled her up into the duct with no trouble. "This is only halfway. We need to be up yet another level. Think you can do it again?"

She didn't say anything, but her eyes were wide as she nodded.

Their next maneuver was a little trickier. They had to shimmy through the ductwork to reach the next floor without being seen.

This time he urged her to climb up his body and stand on his shoulders in order to go through the metal tunnel. Nikki looked unsure, but stepped lightly on his knees and then on his shoulders, and she did it without complaints. In minutes they were both sitting inside the ductwork for the next floor, above the maze of hallways and offices.

Of course the ductworks were a giant maze of metal,

too. But there was enough light to see, coming in through the air vents. He reached into the pocket of his pack and took out a red marker.

Handing it to her, he said, "We'll have to crawl, but mark an arrow midway up the metal every time you turn a corner. We'll try to make only right turns. That way we shouldn't have any trouble finding our way back."

"I don't want to come back. Not without my child. And I don't think we can fit all the boys into the ducts."

"Let's just find them first. Then I'll worry about getting them out. In the meantime, I want you to wait here while I go contact Tarik. I should be able to communicate with him from the next floor up."

"I can't stand to wait. Not when I'm this close. Please let me go."

He pressed his lips together, torn between wanting to keep her safe and letting her go ahead without him. "All right. But go slowly and make no noise. Stop at every vent and check each room. Make sure you leave the marks so I can find you."

She touched a hand to his cheek. "Thank you, Shakir. Thank you for believing in me and bringing me this far. I don't know what I would've done without you."

His cheek burned where her hand lay. His throat closed. He reached up and placed his palm against her hand.

Finally he saw the look in her eyes. "I see what you're thinking. Do *not,* under any circumstances, try this rescue alone, Nik. If you find the boys before I return, wait for me. My life would be worthless if I lost you. And where would your son be if you died? He has no one else."

* * *

This cramped place was all wrong for a confession. And the timing was ridiculous. But it had to be now.

"William has someone else," Nikki told him softly. "He has a father."

Shakir sat back on his heels and stared at her. "I thought…"

"*You* are William's father." There, that wasn't so hard. Except for the sudden hard look in Shakir's eyes.

"I know this is a surprise, but I've been trying to find a way to tell you." She raced ahead, the words tumbling from her mouth. "I'm sorry you didn't know before, but I…"

Shakir put out his hand to stop her. "I understand. No need to say more." The way he was looking at her made her feel small. "Nothing's going to happen to you, Nik, I swear it. But if it makes you feel better, I would have no qualms about becoming your boy's guardian if necessary. You don't have to worry. I'd take care of him as if he were my own son."

He thought she was lying? "Shakir, listen, please."

Turning away, Shakir spoke quietly over his shoulder. "Don't get into any trouble until I return. If you find William, just hold on. I won't be long. Stay safe."

And then he was gone, moving away into the dusky light of the air duct.

A full parade of emotions marched over her, one sentiment at a time. Frustration. Anger. Disappointment. And finally, complete incredulity.

She wanted to yell. Wanted to scream at his retreating figure and forget the damned circumstances. But she kept her mouth shut for her son's sake.

Shakir didn't believe her. She'd waited so long, all

those years, afraid to tell him. And for days she'd been dreaming of which words she could use and what his reaction would be. Now that she'd told him the truth, she was faced with this ridiculous development. What could she do to convince him?

Sitting there, muttering under her breath, she wondered which of them was crazy. Wouldn't a normal man either dread the idea of fatherhood or totally accept it? When a man was told the truth as she had told Shakir, wouldn't he at least entertain the idea? Or perhaps deny it outright? Or at least want to know more?

In this case, he'd seemed to treat the whole idea as not a serious possibility. But why?

She had never lied to Shakir before. One of the things they'd always had between them was honesty. Why would he suddenly, automatically, assume she'd lied to him?

The whole thing seemed surreal. What was going on inside the man that she didn't know?

Nikki had to shake her head to stop the questions. This introspection wasn't bringing her any closer to her son.

After she and Shakir rescued the children and saw them out of Zabbarán to safety... After William was peacefully asleep in his own bed... Nikki swore she and Shakir would revisit this discussion. And she would get to the bottom of his problem.

Taking another moment to gather her wits, she went back to her knees and crawled off into the maze of air ducts. She needed to find her son. He was real. No question. And she could feel his presence somewhere nearby.

* * *

"I'm of two minds on this." Tarik's voice was coming in clear. "Either the Taj are supremely overconfident—or this is a trap."

This was no trap. Shakir felt positive the Taj weren't smart enough to set up anything tricky. But he said nothing in response to his brother's remarks.

"We've had men watching the airstrip twenty miles outside of town," Tarik went on. "The elder Umar has just arrived and boarded a jeep. He is riding in a caravan, coming this way fast. I can't believe he would take that much risk in the face of a potential guerrilla attack on his pet projects. But maybe I underestimate him."

"It's impossible to underestimate Umar." But that didn't mean that they could ignore Captain Baghel's influence. "Have you worked out a different way to move these children to safety?"

Their first plan had relied on sneaking the boys out the same way he and Nikki had come in—through the mine shaft. But now that they knew the kids were being held deep within the ground in the midst of a construction project, they needed to find another solution.

"The only possibility involves a degree of risk I'm not sure you want to take."

"A diversion or decoys?" Shakir didn't like the odds on either one. "I know that's all we have left to use. What are you thinking?"

"To start, my intention is to blow their airstrip and the parked aircraft. That should send many of their soldiers running toward the commotion. Then I plan to close access to both roads in and out of Kuh using dynamite we stole from them."

Shakir could see a couple of big holes in Tarik's plan.

He voiced the first one. "Not bad as far as diversions go. But that still doesn't allow for moving the little boys out via the iron ore tunnel."

"That plan is definitely off. I'm also moving to blow the tunnel shortly after the first explosions at the airfield. After that, the whole area around that building will begin to implode. When everywhere the soldiers look is in chaos, we'll set the choppers down right on the facility grounds and scoop up the kids before the Taj even come to their senses and realize what's going on."

The Taj had little sense, Shakir knew, but this plan had some major drawbacks. "I'm sure I can protect the kids from the explosions, especially if you can send a couple of men into the building to help carry them out."

"Done. I already have you on GPS. I'm amazed, but it's working even underground." Tarik hesitated then asked, "I hear a big *but* in what you're not saying, brother. What's on your mind?"

"The Taj could easily double the guard on the children at the first sign of trouble. Twice the guard means some of them will stick with the kids no matter what. How are we going to move them out of this building then?"

Tarik blew out a breath. "That could be a hiccup in the plan. But I don't believe it will be a problem as soon as the entire building begins imploding around them. I have two men setting charges deep within the earth under the mine tunnel as we speak. Judging by satellite photos, I'm hoping we can make a direct impact on the centrifuge."

Shakir wondered if Tarik had brought enough explosives with him. "What if the guards try to use the children as shields? Or if the soldiers execute the kids as they're running away?"

"That's the part of the plan you aren't going to like, Shakir. We need another distraction, closer in, and a guard of our own at the place where they're holding the children. I was thinking Nikki—"

"Not a chance in bloody hell. Think again."

"She'd be perfect. I can't imagine a better distraction. Listen to what I have in mind, and then ask Nikki if she'd be willing."

"No. She's desperate. She would agree to anything to save her son, even if it means dying. She's already been trying to arrange for me to adopt her son in case anything happens to her."

"Would you? Adopt someone else's son if she dies?"

"When I learned of their meager circumstances a few days ago, I made the decision right then to pay for his upbringing and schooling. That much is settled. But to answer your real question, no, I can't be his or anyone's father figure. I would never want a boy to model his life on my example."

"Don't sell yourself short. You have a lot to offer as a father."

Shakir shook his head into the darkness, knowing his brother couldn't see and couldn't know the truth. "No, her boy would be better off with a nice, stable couple who could raise him as their own. If such a time comes, I will oversee his welfare from afar."

"It won't come to that," Tarik insisted. "But we have to bring all the children out safely soon. Very soon. Let me tell you my idea and then you can discuss it with Nikki. We don't have much time left."

* * *

Nikki's fingers were raw and bleeding from a thousand tiny cuts. The edges on the molded sheets of aluminum were sharp as razors.

It seemed as if she'd been crawling inside these ducts for hours, making tons of right turns and finding next to nothing. Architectural offices with drafting boards and supplies. Offices made for paper shufflers with their cubbyholes and file cabinets. She'd seen all kinds through the vents. A few of them had been occupied with office or construction workers, but she hadn't seen any soldiers yet.

She reached up and marked another arrow, then turned right into the next duct. The act of setting down her hand on the metal below her caused yet another cut. Sitting back on her bottom, she sucked her finger into her mouth and swore silently.

And then she heard something. What was that noise?

The sound was so soft and distant, she could almost swear it was the wind sighing through the air vents. But it wasn't. That was a child's whimper, she just knew it.

Excited to be finally nearing her goal, Nikki twisted around inside the duct and headed off to the left.

The more vents she checked, the more careful she was. At last, through the vent directly ahead, she heard tiny whispered cries. She went flat on her stomach and peered through the vent.

Below her was a room set up like a break room, with lockers and cots. A little boy was sleeping on a cot where she could see him clearly. He was not her son, but she wanted to reach out and touch this child. Shake him. Lift him up to the air duct and ask where the other children—where William was being held.

But he slept soundly. Too soundly perhaps. Had they drugged the children like they'd drugged the women in Umar's harem? The idea sickened her. Still, she couldn't take her eyes off the child.

He whimpered again and tried to roll over in his sleep. That's when she noticed it. A chain attached to the boy's arm and then wrapped around one of the lockers.

She put her hand over her mouth to keep from crying out over the injustice. The horror.

Oh, God. The Taj had drugged and chained the children!

Chapter 13

*W*here was she?

He'd followed the red arrows through the maze of air ducts but all of a sudden they'd stopped. To his knowledge, she hadn't been foolish enough to attempt a solitary rescue. No alarm bells had rung. No loud orders were calling out.

So where was she?

All his searching had given him a better understanding of the geography of the offices. The air duct maze reminded him of the many isolated canyons and switchbacks he'd learned to navigate as a teen in the desert. But time was ticktocking away. Checking his watch, he knew it wouldn't be long before Tarik's explosions would begin. He needed to find Nikki now.

Then he heard a slight rustling coming from the

northwest quadrant where he had not yet searched. Moving fast, he went straight toward it.

By the time Shakir reached her in the vast maze of air ducts, Nikki looked frantic. Her eyes were wild. Blood had seeped through the dress on her back again. And the scarf over her head had pulled loose and hung in disarray around her neck.

She looked so beautiful to his eyes that it simply shocked his mind blank. An inopportune flash of sexual awareness stirred in his groin. Bloody bad timing.

"You've been gone forever. I thought you'd left me."

He pulled her into his arms. "I said I would be back. You forgot the red marks. What happened?"

"William. I can't find William. I've located the room with three other boys about his age, but not my son."

"We'll find him." Shakir wanted to hug her close, to give her strength, but she jerked away from him. She didn't want his sympathy. She needed his help.

Shakir studied her a little closer in the dim light. Her eyes were puffy, with deep purple stains underneath. Her body was bruised and her hands and arms were bloodied by tiny cuts. She had been through too much. He wanted to carry her away from all this, but he knew she wouldn't budge without her son.

A hot possessive rush flooded over him, leaving him a little shell-shocked.

The last thing he wanted was to tell her Tarik's plan. But they had no time left to hesitate.

"Before you show me where the boys are being held, I need to tell you what Tarik has planned."

Nikki looked up at him with such respect and hope,

it tore him in two. The picture she made threatened to clog his throat.

She'd asked him once why he'd never married. He hadn't told her the whole truth, that he wanted marriage. Badly. But only with her. He wanted to give her more children and be there for her grandchildren. He wanted to share her life always.

At this pivotal moment, when lives could be lost or changed forever, he wished he could tell her that. But it would be better for her if she never knew. He was no good for her or her son. That's all she needed to know.

For now, he just had to make sure they both lived through the next couple of hours.

"Tarik's men are sneaking into the facility now and should be entering this building within the next fifteen minutes."

Her eyes betrayed her relief, but it was short-lived.

"It's up to us to free the children and gather them in a safe place near the stairwell."

"How? I couldn't even figure out how to come down out of these ducts to reach them without causing enough noise to bring the entire squad of soldiers running."

He'd known she would attempt a rescue on her own. Shakir was grateful she'd been stymied by the aluminum sheeting. Small favors of fate, but much appreciated.

"I'll show you how. For now we need to talk about the other part of Tarik's plan. Are you willing to do what it takes to make sure all the boys live?"

"Of course. Tell me."

"Tarik is planning on blowing up this building, maybe the whole mountain, starting from the bottom up."

Her eyes grew wide—terrified. To her credit she

remained silent, though her hands began trembling again.

"In a while," he continued, "you will begin to hear bombs going off in the distance. We hope that alone will draw many of the soldiers away from the building. But I'm afraid that not every one of the Taj will leave their post and go.

"We'll need to provide another momentary distraction." This was the part of the plan that he hated. "One of us needs to act as a decoy and give Tarik's men enough time to spirit the children out of harm's way."

She clasped her hands in front of her body as though in prayer. "What do you want me to do?"

He laid out his brother's plan, though it killed him to do so. And he wasn't surprised when she agreed.

She only had one request. "May I make sure William is safely with the other children before I begin my part?"

"Certainly. I'll need your help to round them up. You come with me first because we might have to carry any that are drugged too soundly. Will that do?"

"One more thing." She took his hand. "I want you to promise you'll stay with the children. Do not come back for me. I'll be fine. It won't be that long. I'll be right behind you when everything blows."

Shakir could see the truth all over her face. She didn't believe she was going to live through this. And he couldn't absolutely guarantee that she would. But he would die trying to see to her survival.

"After Tarik's men arrive, I'll…"

"No, Shakir." She shook her head firmly. "Promise me you'll stay with my…our…son. Protect him. Protect all the babies. You have to live to be your son's father. Promise or I refuse to take part in your plan."

He opened his mouth to try again. She couldn't believe he would actually agree to live while she died? But the expression on her face told him it was useless to argue.

Hanging his head, he reluctantly nodded his acceptance. He had to hope that God would forgive his unspoken lie.

"Fine. Now show me how we're going to reach the children. We're almost out of time."

Nikki didn't believe Shakir's idea to squeeze through one of the air vents to reach the children would work. But he'd pointed out a double wide vent located in the maintenance lobby next to the elevators and then had spent only minutes removing the grate and lowering himself through.

Now, almost three minutes later, she still hadn't found William and her nerves were shot as they backtracked through the maze of offices below the ducts. Shakir said he would have no trouble at all finding the rooms where the children were being held.

Still, at any moment they might run into guards. She held her breath and hoped to find William soon.

Suddenly a shout went out. She twisted around to see if they'd been spotted but found nothing but empty hall.

Shakir grabbed her up and stepped inside one of the offices, turning off the overhead light and closing the door most of the way behind them. He watched around the partially closed door until the sound of running could be heard from down the hall. Closing the door completely, he shook his head to indicate she shouldn't move or breathe. Then he waited until the noise of booted footsteps pounded down the hall past the door.

"That should be the alarm alerting the soldiers to the first explosions at the airstrip and on the roads." Shakir peeked out into the hall and then turned back to her. "We don't have a lot of time left. But there's one more thing."

Withdrawing his handgun, Shakir made sure it was loaded and then placed it in her hands. "Only use this in the worst circumstance. The noise will draw a crowd and you won't have enough bullets to take them all out."

Nikki accepted his gun and stashed it in her belt, partially covering it with excess material from her shortened dress. She understood what he'd been saying between the lines. If she was caught and all was lost, one bullet would make sure she was never tortured. A hard, determined swallow was all she allowed herself before she turned to follow Shakir out into the hall.

But he stopped again at the door, turned and lasered a quick kiss across her lips. His kiss was everything. Every unsaid sentiment. Every dream of a future.

Pulling back, he gazed deep into her eyes. "I love you, Nik. Stay alive for my sake."

She couldn't speak, emotion clogged her throat.

He nodded, spun around and led them straight to the break room where three of the boys were being held. Nikki was astounded when Shakir made short work of the chains imprisoning the boys. On two of them, he picked the locks. While on the third, he took something that looked like a tiny piece of pre-chewed gum from his pack and pasted it to the metal chain. Almost immediately, a quiet explosion of light flashed and then the chain just fell away. She let out a breath and made sure the little boy, whose expression seemed beyond rattled, was physically okay. He was crying but uninjured.

She quieted him down; telling him his mummy was waiting for him. Meanwhile, she set to work waking the other children. One of them came awake calling for mamá. Nikki's heart ripped a little at his words. But she shushed him and rubbed the two boys' arms and legs so they could stand on their own. The third child was too groggy and could not be awoken.

"Let's go." Shakir tenderly picked up the sleeping boy. "Can those two walk?"

Both boys nodded as they stared up dumbfounded at the giant man holding their friend. Nikki reminded them that they were leaving this terrible place and to make no noise.

"Hurry then." Shakir went to the door and checked the hall. "It's clear, but we have to go now. Quietly."

Nikki pulled both the boys to her sides, shielding them with her body as she followed Shakir into the hall. The sounds of men shouting could still be heard from elsewhere in the maze of rooms. Both of her little charges were frightened into silence.

It was the hardest thing she'd ever had to do, but Nikki turned away from the direction where she thought William must be and hurried the little boys down the empty hallways, heading toward the stairwell. When they hit the maintenance lobby, Shakir picked up the other two boys and tucked all three under his arms as he pounded down the stairs.

Nikki hated the idea of taking these innocents down instead up into the fresh air. But Shakir had been right when he said down was the only direction where the children would not be easily discovered as the guards searched for them. And while she went back up to find William.

On the next floor down, they opened the lobby door to the big, unfinished space just as two of Tarik's men dropped out of the air duct in the corner. Startled at first, she took Shakir's silence for a sign that these men were friends. With no words, the two men took charge of the three boys as she and Shakir turned around to sneak back up to the office floor.

William. He was all she could think about now.

She and Shakir eased into the maze of hallways once again. Following in his steps for only a few seconds, she stopped as he listened at one door. He tried the knob but it was locked.

Without a second's hesitation, Shakir used his knife point and picked the lock. The man was simply amazing. She was still shaking her head at his versatility when she entered the room—and saw William. Her baby.

She ran to him and shook him awake.

"*Maman?* Is it really you?"

Taking him in her arms and hugging him to her breast, she had to fight off the tears. "Yes, William, it's Mummy. I'm here to take you home, but you must be very quiet. Can you?"

"Is it a game?" He leaned away from her and opened his eyes wider. "I don't like it here."

Shakir stood behind her, working to free William from his chain. "This isn't a game," he whispered to the boy. "But you must do everything your mother says. Do you understand?"

"Yes, Papa. I will. I'm a good boy."

Nikki knew her son would probably call any man "Papa" if he felt comfortable in his presence. But she'd noticed Shakir stumble at William's use of the term. However, the glorious man never stopped working for one second. Soon all the boys were freed and then Shakir checked the hall again.

"Everything looks quiet." Shakir took a breath. "But…"

"I know what I must do, Shakir." She gathered all three of the boys to her. "I'm leaving first, children. You must follow Shakir. Walk out on your own, going the way he shows you but without saying a word. He will make sure you can all go home. Back to your mothers. Okay?"

Two of the boys nodded solemnly though one of them began weeping softly. William wasn't having any of it. He shook his head and grabbed for her neck.

"No, *Maman*. I want to go with you."

She closed her eyes, praying for the strength to do what she must.

Prying her baby's thin little arms off her neck, she spoke softly. "You have to go with Papa. Do what he says. *Maman* will come for you as soon as she can. Be a good boy now and remember to be very quiet."

Shakir gently took William's hand. "He will be a good boy for you. He promised."

The loving look on Shakir's face nearly broke her in two. But she bit her lip and stepped away, going straight for the hallway door without looking back. Time was not on their side and she had made a promise, too.

"Brother. This child…" Tarik pointed to William. "He looks like… Is it possible?"

Still astonished at the resemblance between Nikki's son and his own childhood pictures, Shakir could barely answer. "I… Yes, it is a possibility. Take him. Hurry."

"But you're supposed to come with us. Now, Shakir. We don't have…"

Tarik's words were cut short as the floor under their feet shook. The first underground explosion! No. It was too soon.

"Take these three to safety with the others. I'm going back for Nikki. We'll be right behind you."

Shakir had no doubt that Tarik would save the boys—his son. *His son.* The idea was almost too much to accept.

But he should've known Nikki would never lie to him. Their past experience should have told him as much. Of the two of them, he was the one who stretched the truth or left out enough of the truth to qualify as a lie. Not her. Never her.

A little queasy, Shakir bent down and embraced his son. "This is your uncle Tarik, William. Go with him. Remember what your mother said."

"Yes, Papa. But I want my *maman*. Will you get her for me?"

With blurry eyes, Shakir bit down on his lip before speaking. "I'll bring her to you, son. I promise."

"Shakir." Tarik put a hand on his arm and whispered in his ear. "You're out of time. Nikki will have to find her own way out. The elder Umar is on his way down in the public elevator. We have to leave before we're discovered."

He shook off his brother's hand. "I'm not going without her. Take these last three children and go now."

Tarik grabbed William's hand and started for the

back stairs but Shakir stopped him momentarily. "If we don't make it, raise my son to be like you. Swear it."

"I will take care of him for you, brother. I promise."

For one more second, Shakir stood and watched as William went up the stairs with Tarik. His child. His son.

Choked with emotion, Shakir turned and walked back into the unfinished room, heading for the open air duct. He thought it was a very good thing that he didn't have time to wonder what being a father would be like. It was beyond his imagination so he managed to clear the dream from his mind, concentrating instead on developing a plan to reach Nikki and bring them both to safety.

He refused to let her die at the hands of the Taj Zabbar. Not a chance in hell. He had too much to tell her. To explain.

As he lifted himself into the open air duct and swung up to the next level, Shakir's mind was racing. Where was she? What had…?

The sound of a distant shouting put him on alert as he crawled toward the offices where he'd spotted the soldiers congregating earlier. He couldn't move fast enough. He felt as if he were crawling through water.

And then it happened. The thing he had most hoped to avoid. The one thing that could change everything.

A shot rang out. And his heart stopped.

Chapter 14

With her hands raised high above her head, Nikki slowly turned around in the hallway to face the shooter. She'd almost made it as far as the stairwell. Just a few more steps and she would've been gone. She knew the shot had only been a warning, the bullet whizzing over her head. But she was obviously finished with being a decoy.

She'd spent at least fifteen minutes racing through the maze of hallways, teasing the guards by showing a glimpse of herself and then disappearing. Nikki prayed Shakir had managed to save William and the other boys in the time she'd given them. She hadn't really expected to save herself.

But she had expected that one of the soldiers would've used his rifle to try stopping her long before now. As she turned to face the shooter, she realized what was

different about him. The soldier holding the rifle trained
to the middle of her chest was some kind of officer. She
could tell by his uniform and medals.

He yelled at her in the Taj language. But when she
kept staring at him, he tried speaking in French.

"Do not move." The officer came closer, peering
at her down the barrel of his rifle. "Who or what are
you?"

"I am…" Before she could answer, the whole building
shook and the lights flickered.

The officer glanced up toward the fluorescents and
then narrowed his eyes as he looked back to her. She
closed her own eyes, quite sure her end was on the way.
While waiting for the bullet she was sure would kill her,
thoughts of Shakir and her son flashed in her mind.

Would they miss her? Would Shakir tell their son
what she had done to save his life? Would Shakir eventually find another lover to be his wife and care for their
child?

Moments passed and nothing happened. Then the
sound of elevator doors sliding back caused her to blink
open her eyes and take a breath. She couldn't see the
public elevators from where she stood. But the officer
with the rifle turned, saluting to someone out of her line
of sight. Should she try running again?

Before she could make the decision, heavy footsteps
pounded down the hall, coming in her direction.

More words in Taj were spoken. Questions asked and
answered. The officer turned and gestured to her.

A middle-aged man walked into her view and stood
beside the officer. The new man was well dressed with a
salt-and-pepper beard and sideburns. He looked vaguely
familiar.

Nikki was trying to place him when he turned and spoke. "Ah, there you are," the man said in English. "Somewhat the worse for wear, I see. I have some questions for you, my dear."

Trying to swallow, Nikki's pulse raced and her mouth went dry. She suddenly knew that this must be Umar, the man who had kidnapped her and her son and then put them both into prisons.

Hatred sprang up in her heart. Cold and gray and dangerous.

But she fought the life-threatening emotion, knowing that hatred would make her sloppy. She needed to remain calm and think clearly. Thinking was the only possible way she would ever make it out of here alive. And she desperately wanted to live long enough to see Shakir and William, to tell them that she loved them once more.

Umar spoke arrogantly. "Where are the children?"

Nikki shrugged a shoulder and raised her eyebrows. The elder wouldn't like not getting an answer to his question, she knew. But she wasn't at all prepared for what happened next.

He pulled a handgun from his jacket pocket. Again she held her breath and waited for her fate.

But Umar spun around and calmly pulled the trigger, hitting his officer squarely in the forehead. The man crumpled to the ground. Dead in that instant.

What on earth? Had the officer so disappointed the elder that he deserved to die? Was she next? Her shoulders came up and she fisted her hands, ready to run.

Umar turned back to her. "You feel sorry for Captain Baghel? Don't. Before the end of today you may wish for such an easy a death. Take heed."

Umar made a threatening move in her direction.

"Now, back to where you were ready to give me answers. I was not pleased about losing you and the other females from my harem. And I was extremely unhappy that one of my wives was taken out the country against her will. But the children—that is another matter altogether. I *will* have those children returned. Or else."

"Why should I know where they are?" She wanted to smile at him. To make him believe she was telling the truth and wasn't worried. But her lips trembled so badly that she couldn't make them do as she commanded:

"You think I am stupid?" Instead of roaring his anger, Umar's voice was low and cool like a rasp of the snake. "You think I can be fooled into imagining this is some sort of coincidence? I should kill you right now for being disrespectful."

She shook her head hard enough to give herself a headache. "Not at all. I know you are a smart man. But children can be so difficult. Perhaps we can make a deal."

Umar's eyes turned black and narrowed into slits. "What kind of deal?"

She opened her mouth to offer her own freedom and the possibility of the return of his wife in exchange for the children's freedom. But before she could get the words out, the building rolled under her feet again and the sound of underground rumbling made it clear what was happening. Little pieces of plaster and a fine dust sprayed down on both of their heads.

Umar ducked then looked up, assuring himself that the ceiling was not coming down upon his head. But at that very moment the air vent behind him exploded. When the plaster dust cleared an instant later, Shakir appeared at the hole where the vent had been and jumped down into the hallway.

Shakir? Oh, no. He'd promised to stay away and rescue the children. The only reason she wasn't already hysterical was because she had believed he was long gone and safe. She was stunned and immobilized by the sight of him.

But Umar wasn't immobile. He moved fast. Reaching out, he grabbed her around the neck and pulled her close to his chest. Backing them both down the hallway away from Shakir, he jammed the barrel of his gun into her temple.

"One of the Kadir sons?" Umar growled his disapproval. "I should have known your family would be behind this. And I should have smelled the stench long before you appeared. It will be a pleasure to kill you where you stand, dog."

Shakir's lips narrowed into a grimace. "Don't be hasty, you may need me, Your Excellency."

Those last words were spit out with obvious sarcasm. But considering the tight way Umar was holding her, Nikki didn't dare open her mouth to make a remark. Had it been otherwise, she would've told Shakir to be quiet. He was asking to die, and she didn't want him dead before she could get her own hands on him for lying about leaving her.

"Let her go." Shakir took a threatening step in their direction.

In a blink, Umar turned the gun toward Shakir and fired.

Ohmygod! He shot him!

Shakir felt the sting of a bullet entering and leaving his upper right arm. He stopped moving forward as blood oozed through his shirtsleeve. Putting the fingers of his left hand to the wound, he assured himself of what he'd known to be true. It was merely a flesh wound. The bullet had gone right through. The wound would bleed, but not badly.

He decided not to let Umar know that the bullet wound was only superficial. Making a big show of wincing in pain, Shakir cradled his perfectly fine arm to his chest.

"Don't be impatient, Umar," he said through gritted teeth. "Can't we talk? I heard you say you might be willing to deal. Deal with me."

"Deal? With what? You have nothing I want."

"I have the children."

Umar's face went hard. The anger shimmered off him like a cool summer shower against heated rocks. Shakir was glad the man was pointing his gun at him and not at Nikki.

"Where are they?" Umar's voice shook. "I have been promised a large fortune if I deliver those boys to eastern Europe by tomorrow. A deal is still possible. You Kadirs are supposed to be such wonderful traders. How much do you want to take the children to the buyer?"

"I want the woman." Shakir tilted his head toward Nikki.

"This piece of skin and bones?" Umar jerked her tighter against him and put the gun back to her temple.

Shakir drew in a breath, fighting the testosterone raging in his bloodstream along with a reckless urge to kill the elder. The man with his hands on Nikki. Hurting her.

Shakir's vision blurred into a red haze. His palms itched to squeeze the life out of the asshole Umar.

But Shakir knew he couldn't jump the elder and kill him without the possibility of Nikki dying, too. Trying to still the savage beast within him scratching to get out, Shakir kept his mouth shut and his body quiet.

"Oh, is that how it is then? This entire debacle was my mistake for taking the wrong woman? But how was I to know she belonged to a Kadir when she showed up in Zabbarán looking for work? But then again," Umar added with a wry grin, "knowing about her might not have mattered very much in the total scheme of things. She was a very beautiful woman, after all. However, in retrospect, I certainly would have added extra security."

Umar actually let out a giggle. The blighter. His crazed laughter sounded much like that of the jackal. The noise made Shakir's skin crawl and the temptation to jump the elder grew nearly impossible to ignore.

Shakir sidestepped like a prizefighter and inched backward, worried that Umar would simply kill Nikki outright just to spite him. But then Shakir made a huge mistake. He held out his hands, palms up, trying to keep the elder calm. It was a sure sign of weakness and Umar spotted it immediately.

This time when the elder's weapon exploded, Shakir took the bullet in his right thigh. The pain was white-hot and searing. When he looked down, all he could see was blood.

The bastard had shot Shakir again! Nikki screamed and screamed. She couldn't stop. Watching the man she loved in horrible pain and slowly dying was much worse than dying herself.

"Shut up, whore! You've caused me enough trouble." Umar struck her in the temple with the butt of his gun.

She stumbled to her knees, seeing blinding white spots in front of her eyes. Once again she expected the end of her life to come next. Instead, the tile beneath her suddenly rolled with another one of Tarik's explosions. This time, the whole building rumbled and large chunks of ceiling plaster dropped on top of all of them. She put her hands over her head to protect herself.

When the haze cleared a bit, she saw Umar dropping to one knee and lifting his gun. Looking up, she realized Shakir was limping steadily toward them through the chaos. Why was Shakir still coming at him? The man she loved had a big, bleeding hole in his thigh. Why didn't he go the other direction?

Nikki fumbled at her waist for the gun Shakir had given her. By the time she had it out and ready to fire at Umar, though, she could see Umar's finger already on his trigger and he was pointing the gun toward Shakir.

She watched in horror as the elder pulled the trigger, but nothing happened. The gun misfired. Umar looked down at the weapon in his hand and swore. But it was too late.

Shakir was upon him.

Roaring with anger, Shakir picked Umar up and lifted him over his head. It was a stunning feat of pure power and Nikki was amazed that any human could have such strength after having been shot twice. Umar looked like a rag doll, limp limbs and arms askew. Then Shakir slammed the elder up against the wall with such force, the building shook again.

Nikki winced as she heard Umar's bones cracking.

Shakir groaned and dropped the elder to the tile floor. The limp man skidded a distance down the hall. After his body stopped sliding, Umar made a small noise, then fell silent. Shakir took a step toward the heap of vile humanity on the floor as though he would like to make sure the job was finished. But then, thankfully, Shakir stopped, turned again and rushed to kneel beside her.

"Are you hurt badly?"

"No." Her voice was as shaky as she felt. "But you are. The blood is pouring out of that wound on your leg." She could barely look at it. The sight of all that blood made her stomach roil.

She could hear the distant explosions coming one after another now, but her thoughts centered on how to stop the bleeding before Shakir lost too much blood. She tried ripping the slashed bottom of her dress. But before she made any headway, Shakir pulled the Bedouin scarf from out of his pack and handed it to her.

"Press this tightly against my wound while I cut a strip from your dress." He pulled the big knife out of its holster on his uninjured thigh and sliced the seam of what was left of her dress with precision.

Nikki couldn't imagine how he could still be clear-headed, what with all the blood loss and the loud sounds and the shaking of the building around them. She forced herself to concentrate on leaning against the gunshot wound with all her might. Shakir winced as she pressed down, but he kept working. Her admiration and respect for his strength kept her from becoming hysterical.

In a few moments, he had a long narrow strip cut

from her dress and was tying it around his leg over the wound. "I need a little help," he said.

She did as he told her and held the scarf compressed in place as he tied down the strip. It was hard to believe he could take the pressure over such a wound.

"Let me put antiseptic on it." She was terrified that he was dying. But she would do everything in her power to keep him alive.

"No time," he said as he came to his left knee and attempted to stand. "We have to get out of here now. The whole building should be coming down any minute."

His foot slid out from under his body and he went down on his good knee with a hard thud. Looking up at her, he grinned with one of those sweet, sensible grins that always made her heart rate speed up.

"Looks like this is as far as I go," he said with a cough. "Get out of the building. Run up the stairs and then make your way behind the drain pipe. Tarik should still have a chopper there to pick you up."

She took hold of his arm. "Nonsense. I'm not leaving without you. Lean on me."

Shakir shook his head. "I'm too heavy. Leave me. Go. Live. Be our son's mother."

Tugging on him, she leaned over and adjusted his arm around her shoulders. "Quit griping and come on. We go together or we don't go at all."

Nikki saw the moment it registered with him that she meant what she said. A bleak nod replaced the sweet grin. But he did put his weight on the good leg and managed to stand on his one good foot. Once upright, he seemed to catch a second wind and wrapped his arm tighter around her shoulders.

"All right, princess. Let's see how you get me up those stairs."

She started down the hall slowly, pulling and pushing and cajoling him along. "If you haven't noticed, I'm not a princess anymore. Far from it. But I am the woman who is going to make sure you live through all this. Now save your strength and help me."

When they'd reached the end of the hall and were almost to the maintenance lobby and the stairs, she turned her head to check on Umar. His body still lay where it fell. If she'd had the chance to, she would've gone back to check on whether he was still alive. But as she and Shakir limped around the corner, yet another explosion rocked the floor and the walls started to crumble. The ceiling above the hallway that they'd left collapsed with a mighty eruption of plaster dust. Now she could only hope Umar was already dead.

The lights flickered and went out. She held her breath until emergency lights embedded in the floors came on and illuminated everything in an eerie glow.

"Hurry up," she begged Shakir, though she imagined her pleas for speed were useless. He was barely limping on his bad leg and she was too weak to take any more of his weight.

They reached the stairwell. But smoke and a fine dust were already rising from the floors below, cloaking the way ahead. Tears suddenly clouded her vision, mixing salty water with dry fear. They were going to die here in this Taj building. She prayed to God that Shakir's brothers would raise her son and learn to love him as a nephew.

"I thought you wanted to hurry?" Shakir dragged her

closer to his body and held her tight just as they reached the first step.

This was an impossible task. She saw that now. How would he ever make it up two flights on one leg? She almost sat down and gave up.

But Shakir reached out with both his hands and grabbed hold of the banister. "Hang on to my belt," he ordered, fisting his hands tightly around the smooth metal.

She couldn't imagine what he had in mind but she stepped directly behind him and entwined her fingers around his utility belt. What he did next was nothing short of a miracle. He literally dragged his body up the stairs by using upper arm strength alone—

Well, that and an amazing show of pure determination.

They made it to the ground level, but with only seconds to spare. The stairs below began to sway and cave in.

Shrieking as she jumped off the top stair, she barely gained her footing when that last stair rattled and then crashed into the black abyss. The modern shell of a lobby began crumbling around them, too. Shakir gritted his teeth and lifted her off her feet from his bad side.

"Put me down. This is too hard for you. Let me walk."

"Quiet. We're out of time." Running on what she figured was pure adrenaline, he dragged both her and his bad leg outside into the lavender-and-rose glow of another dawn.

Nikki could hear shouting and gunshots in the distance. But the air was filling with choking red dust and soon she couldn't see more than five feet ahead.

Shakir seemed to know exactly where he was headed. So she tried to make out the sounds around them as he zigzagged through the haze. The one sound she'd hoped to hear, the noise made by helicopter rotors, was conspicuously missing.

She prayed that her son and the other boys were all safely away from this place. But had Tarik's men left without her and Shakir?

If they were too late to catch a helicopter ride, she wondered if Shakir could find his way back through the mine shaft tunnel. It wouldn't be easy to negotiate that space again with his leg, but it was a far better option than standing here and being shot.

As Shakir ducked underneath the timbers holding up the drain, she felt yet another giant rumble as the earth began to sway to and fro. The whole mountain must be coming down and their tunnel would collapse. They were free of the underground building, but they still might not live through this. The entire town of Kuh Friez might not survive.

Suddenly she heard engine sounds above the din. Glancing up, she spotted a black chopper flying down the mountainside, running only fifteen to twenty feet off the ground and following the line of the drain pipe. Whoever was at the controls of that craft was one hell of a pilot.

"There's Tarik." Shakir set her on her feet and pulled the earbud and mic from his pack. He used the clicker on his microphone to signal his brother.

Winds swirled and dust rose around her, blowing the scarf off her head and burning her skin, as the chopper hovered directly above them. They were saved.

The chopper flew lower, closer and closer, until she

could see Tarik hanging from the door with his arm outstretched, beckoning her to climb aboard.

She turned to Shakir. "You first."

"Move," he screamed above the engine noise.

She shook her head. She was not going without him.

He cursed, then reached out with one hand and grabbed her around the waist. Linking arms with Tarik, he let his brother pull him onboard with her dangling by his side.

Before she was completely inside the chopper, she was already letting out a huge sigh of relief. They were going to live. Everything would be all right.

But out of her peripheral vision she saw something striking the side of the chopper near her head. She turned her face to see what had happened while Shakir worked to close the door and drag her fully inside. But as her chin swivelled back, she felt something like the sting of a bee hitting her cheek.

She didn't have time to cry out, because in that instant, everything went black.

Chapter 15

When Nikki managed to pry open her heavy eyelids, she found herself looking up into the eyes of Shakir's brother Tarik. She knew she was lying flat on her back, and she could hear the drumming of the chopper's engine. But her head was fuzzy about details.

Disappointed that it was Tarik leaning over her and not Shakir, she fought to focus on what had happened. She remembered the sharp pain and not much else. Next, she tried to sit up but couldn't. Light-headed and queasy, she could barely raise her head. The pounding pain in her temple felt like someone was driving a sharp poker into her skull.

"You're going to be okay," Tarik told her above the engine noise as he moved something beside her head. "Lie still. You've been shot and you may be going into shock."

"William?"

Tarik's mouth actually came up in a half smile. "He's fine. Safe. So are the other boys. He'll be at the hospital when you arrive."

"Shakir?"

A gray shadow passed in front of Tarik's face, and Nikki's stomach rolled again. "Is he alive?"

"So far." Another voice, still not Shakir's, came from right beside her.

She worked hard and finally turned her head enough to look in that direction. Shakir was lying on his back not three feet away and another man was frantically working over him. There were plastic tubes strung up and attached to his arm and liquids were dripping into his veins.

"Shakir!"

"He's out, ma'am. I'm afraid he can't hear you."

"But he will live." He had to live. He couldn't leave her and William again.

The man working over Shakir didn't say a word. She turned back to Tarik. "He will live, won't he?"

"It depends. It's possible."

Shakir? No! He couldn't die after saving her life and the life of her son. She hadn't yet told him she loved him. She hadn't even had the chance to ask her questions and say that she wanted them to make a new life as a family.

Nikki used every bit of her strength to stretch out her arm and take Shakir's hand. Her stomach roiled with the effort and her eyes blurred. But she fought to stay conscious.

"Shakir." Her hoarse voice could barely be heard.

"Shakir, listen to me. I love you. I've always loved you. And William loves you, too. Don't leave us. We need you."

A yellow haze obscured her gaze for a moment. When her eyes cleared, she could swear Shakir was watching her out of his half-closed eyes.

"Fight this, Shakir. Live. Don't give up now that we've made it."

She had to swallow down the bile as it threatened to choke her. "I want us to be a family. Your son needs you." The tears began streaming down her cheeks. "I need you. I don't want to go on without you."

Shakir's mouth opened and he mumbled something that she couldn't understand. But she knew he was hearing her voice.

"Please, darling," she croaked. "Please don't leave me. Not again. I can't… I can't…"

"No good… Forget me…"

Were those real words? Had he really told her to forget him? Now when she'd found him again and he had saved them all? Impossible.

She opened her mouth to plead, but nothing came out. Fighting for words— Fighting for his life— She squirmed, trying to get closer.

"Nikki, settle down. You'll hurt yourself." Tarik's voice captured her attention for the moment and she tilted her head toward him.

But when she turned, the spike that had been driving into her temple suddenly detonated like one of Tarik's explosions. Blinding pain took her breath as the whole world began receding into the foggy, foggy background.

She struggled to stay conscious. To stay with Shakir. But she was too weak. Too helpless. Ultimately, her body shut down.

Shakir forced his eyes open against monumental pain. The last thing he remembered was Nikki's voice begging him to stay alive. He must be still alive, because dead would never hurt this much.

But was she all right? And William?

A son. He had a son. The idea still astounded him.

When his eyes finally cleared enough for him to look at objects nearby, he expected to find Nikki again. Instead, he was clearly in some kind of hospital. He knew the signs. Wires were sticking into various parts of his body and a machine beeped periodically somewhere near his head.

He groaned and tried to open his mouth. Nothing happened. Closing his eyes again, he drifted off.

When Shakir next opened his eyes, he was in the same room. But this time Tarik was sitting beside his bed.

Shakir tried to speak but coughed instead.

Tarik looked up and then jumped to his feet. "You're awake. Good to see you."

"Thirsty…" His voice broke and rasped like steel wool on rusty metal.

Tarik turned to someone else and suddenly a nurse was there holding out a straw. "Here you are, sir. Go slowly. But this should help."

Shakir drained the straw of its cool, soothing liquid. Then he tried again. "Thank you…"

"I'll leave the water beside your bed. If you want more, just ask."

"Tarik."

"Yeah, bro. I'm here."

"Is Nikki…?"

"Very much alive and getting healthier every day. She's in the hospital, but the doctors think she'll be able to leave by tomorrow or the next day. Your son is okay, too. At least physically. Darin and Rylie are taking care of all the boys back at the family's temporary compound in the Mediterranean islands until we can sort out where they belong."

"Where are we?" His head was still spinning and nothing seemed right.

"A Turkish hospital. It was closest place to Zabbarán. But you and Nikki have been getting the best care possible."

"How long have I been here?"

"A week. You were in pretty bad shape when we brought you in."

"So I'm going to live?"

"You're too frigging tough to die, brother. But I'm afraid you are in for a long siege. Rounds of operations and then months of rehab. Still, the doctors are fairly certain you will keep the leg. That was one hell of a good field doctoring job you did on yourself."

He was alive and it looked like he was going to stay that way. Not quite sure how he felt about that yet, Shakir made a sincere effort to remain clearheaded and in the moment. There were things he needed to say.

"Remember your promise? You said you would take care of Nikki and William for me. Does that still hold?"

Tarik looked confused. "Of course. The whole family will pitch in and watch out for them until you are well enough to do it yourself. They ask for you all the time."

Shakir swallowed hard and fought his weak voice. "I need more of your help. Much more. I want them to have everything I own. Have Darin set it up. And I want you to tell Nikki I loved her, but that I didn't make it."

"What? You want me to lie and say you died? You must be delirious. I'm not lying to her about anything."

"Do you care about me?"

Tarik's eyes became hard and his lips curled. "Don't be an ass."

"If you really care about being a good brother like the man I know you are, the same way I care about you, then marry Nikki. Give my son a father. Make him a Kadir."

"Now I know you're delirious. Or just plain insane. Did you hit your head during that rescue?"

"I'm dead serious, Tarik." He was desperate for his brother to understand. "I'm no good for them. They need a decent man who will protect them and cherish them the way they deserve."

"Nikki needs the man who loves her. She needs you, you idiot." Tarik ran his fingers through his hair. "I don't know who you think you are, but she knows. She knows you're the man who saved her and her son's lives. She knows you would never hurt them deliberately and... she loves you.

"That makes you the right man for the job. Not me."

Frustrated and suddenly in a lot more pain, Shakir

couldn't think of any argument that would persuade Tarik. He opened his mouth, but only a groan came out.

"No brother of mine is this much of a coward," Tarik began again, obviously suppressing his anger. "I'll have Darin start on the transfer of property. I agree that might be a good idea in case of any further danger. And I'll put Nikki off for a while by telling her you can't have visitors. But you are responsible for all the rest. For telling her yourself what you want her to know."

"But…"

"That's my only offer. Take it or leave it."

Nikki stood gazing out her kitchen window at the little boys playing in her garden high above the ocean. It was a lovely fall afternoon on the Mediterranean, with the sun shining and a few high cirrus clouds drifting over the cerulean sky. But to her, it was only another in a long line of gray days.

Four months of drab, dull days in fact since she'd last seen Shakir in that helicopter. Every time she thought of those last moments and the intervening months it made her sigh.

He'd refused to see her. For four long, gruelling months, he would not let her visit. Either at his hospital bedside or during his months of rehabilitation. His brothers kept her up with news on how his health was progressing. And they swore they'd delivered all her messages.

Shakir was, as she knew all along, a good man who would honor his responsibilities. He'd asked his family to watch out for her and William, to keep them safe and away from the danger of the Taj Zabbar. And he'd gifted her and their son with all his property and money, including this wonderful two-story home on the Mediterranean coast.

She'd tried to respect his wishes and had accepted his gifts in the name of her son. But Nikki was ready to track Shakir down and make him face her and the son they had made together. If he didn't want them, didn't want the family he had waiting, then he would have to tell her so to her face.

She was certainly ready to give him a few choice words. She and William didn't want Shakir's property without having him, too. The one thing they needed most was Shakir.

Wiping away her tears of frustration, she looked in the distance at the green-and-blue sea and then focused in on the boys kicking the football on the lawn. At one boy in particular. The tallest boy, even though he was not the oldest, was the one with thick dark brown hair and gray-blue eyes. The light of her life.

William was much stronger than she was. He had lived through his weeks in captivity with a rare few side effects. She'd taken him to a psychologist for treatment, but at this point he seemed to need nothing more than love. He amazed her everyday with his balance and quiet strength.

Like his father. Or like the man she'd once imagined Shakir to be.

William had even been the first to suggest that they take in the other lost boys to live with them until their families could be located with the help of the United Nations. She and Darin and his wife, Rylie, were still trying to find the parents for three of the boys. So far, they'd reunited one child with his family in Switzerland. A fourth boy, the Asian-looking one, insisted that he couldn't go home. That his parents were too poor to take him back. Rylie had agreed it was quite likely his parents had sold him to Umar. That sort of thing apparently happened in the Far East all the time.

Nikki's heart went out to the child. He needed a lot of attention, but William was wonderful with him.

She wanted to do much more. During her research, Nikki had discovered many thousands of lost children all over the world—just like these boys. It was heartbreaking, and she'd been mulling over ways to make a difference.

As she considered the possibilities, something appeared in her peripheral vision at the side yard. It was a man. Heading toward the children.

Shakir's brothers had warned her to be careful of strangers. Tarik had even put up a surveillance system with cameras. But it might take too long for anyone to come to their assistance.

Nikki refused to have a gun in the house with children. But she kept Shakir's knife, the big one that had saved her life more than once, nearby at all times.

Reaching high into the cabinet, she grabbed the knife and hurried out the back door in a matter of seconds. By now the man had reached the boys and was talking to them. Talking to William especially.

She ran about fifteen feet before she slowed. There was something about the man that didn't seem as threatening all of a sudden. He was broad-shouldered and might've been tall, but it was difficult to tell because she now saw that he was leaning on a cane.

Ohmygod. The man must be Shakir. It had to be him.

Jolting to a complete stop, Nikki was torn between the need to see the man she loved and the anger building toward him for not telling her he was coming. At just that moment, Shakir turned to look at her as though he had been hearing her thoughts.

So much was written in his expression as he stood watching her that she couldn't separate the longing from the obvious guilt in his eyes. The man was tearing himself in two, and she wanted to know why.

William spotted her where she stood and came running in her direction. "*Maman,* Papa's here! He came. He came to see us."

Slowly, she began walking toward William while keeping her eyes on Shakir not far in the background. Her son had been hearing more about his father recently, through his uncles. And now William must be convinced Shakir was going to stay and be his real father.

Nikki wasn't as sure. But she slid the knife into her dress pocket before William could spot it.

"Will Papa play football with me?" She had never seen William so excited.

"Your father is still injured, son."

William turned to look at Shakir. "Oh. From when he saved us. I know. Well, I can help him. I can hold him up on the bad side. That would be good, wouldn't it, *Maman?*"

Tears filled Nikki's eyes, but she held them back as she reached out for her son and pulled him close. "I need to speak to your father. You can talk to him more a little later. For now, why don't you and the other boys go inside and ask the housekeeper to fix your lunch. I think she was planning on baking cookies."

Her son looked disappointed but he nodded his acceptance. Then he turned and raced for Shakir, hugging him so hard around the middle that the two of them almost toppled to the ground.

Shakir whispered something to him and William nodded again. Finally, her son began gathering up the other boys and they ran off with the promise of cookies after lunch in their minds.

Nikki straightened her shoulders and went to Shakir. "We need to talk."

He tilted his chin and agreed. "Is there somewhere we can sit? This is the first day I've walked this far and…" He shrugged as if he was embarrassed to be in pain.

"Certainly. Over there under the tree." She pointed to the wooden bench in the shade.

Once they were seated together and she felt his warmth at her side, it was all she could do not to wrap herself around him and kiss him senseless. How could he have made them stay apart this long?

But Shakir didn't look like he was ready to kiss and make up. A chill wind off the ocean shivered over her skin, making her doubt his intentions.

Oh, God. What would she do if he told her good-bye?

It was all Shakir could manage to keep his hands off of Nikki. Those long months of dreaming about her had never been as good as the real thing.

But here she was beside him, all soft and silky warm. With the curves in all the right places that he remembered. And with that upturned nose and proud chin that he'd always adored. He had to clasp his hands together to keep from touching her.

"How are you feeling? Does it still hurt very much?"

"Not a lot." He had to pull himself together and say what he'd come to say.

Tarik had called him a coward and Shakir supposed that was what he was. He didn't want to face this. Didn't want to see the look of disappointment in her eyes when she heard him tell her the truth of who he was.

"You're right, Nik. We do have to talk. I need to…" The words clogged up his throat and when he finally forced something out, he said, "Why didn't you tell me before that I was William's father? Why didn't you find me and let me know about the baby?"

He hadn't meant to say that. Why had those been his first words?

Nikki's eyes grew dark and tight. "I tried, damn you. I searched and searched when I found out I was pregnant. Where the hell did you disappear to?"

"You looked for me?" He hadn't expected her to say that. He'd supposed that she'd been grateful not to be burdened with a man like him as a father to her child. And he'd been absolutely positive her parents would be thrilled to be rid of him.

"I nearly killed myself looking for you," she said. "I even found an address for your family and mailed them a letter asking for your whereabouts."

"Did you tell them about the baby?"

She shook her head. "It wasn't any of their business. But I did receive a return letter from Darin saying he hadn't heard from you in months. Where'd you go?"

"I…I…" The time for keeping secrets was over.

He hung his head so he wouldn't have to watch the disappointment in her eyes. "When you told me you were marrying someone else, I was devastated and miserable. At the time, I tried to convince myself that I felt bad because of my hurt pride. But it was more than that. Deep down I was sure you sent me away because you'd decided I wasn't good enough for you. I knew that's what your parents thought, and I tended to agree with them. I wasn't nearly good enough for you."

Nikki remained deadly silent. He wished he knew what she was thinking, but it was time to open up about everything.

"I'm still not good enough, Nik. Nothing's changed in all these years. I'm a killer. You've seen me in action now. You know. I don't feel a thing when I take a life. That makes me a savage and not worthy of being loved."

"Oh, for pity's sake!" Nikki punched him hard on his good arm. "Look at me. Listen to me."

He raised his head until he met her gaze. Those warm hazel eyes of hers were blazing green.

"Answer me this," she demanded. "Have you ever taken a life for fun or profit?"

His stomach churned at the thought. "No, never."

She punched him again. "Of course not. You kill because you or someone you love is in danger. You're not a savage. Far from it. You're a good man who is strong and brave and is prepared to defend the people who matter."

Rolling her eyes, she added, "I would never have fallen in love with a man who enjoyed killing."

"You love me?"

Nikki pulled her arm back, preparing to slug him again, but he captured her fist in both of his hands.

"I told you that in the helicopter, you imbecile." She gave him a sharp nod of her head. "I'm sure you heard me."

He'd thought he dreamed those words. Thought he'd wanted them so badly that he made them up out of his pain.

He reached for her, needing to feel her body next to his heart. But she pulled back.

"So where were you when I went looking? I always figured you were in some other woman's bed."

The chuckle escaped his lips before he could catch it. "Nothing so tame. I couldn't think when you said it was over. I couldn't even look at myself in the mirror. I wasn't any bloody good for anyone and I acted the part. Took myself on a little three week binge. Tore up every bar in London, until finally I landed before a magistrate who gave me a choice. Jail time or enroll in the army. I chose a paratrooper regiment and never looked back."

"You were a British paratrooper?"

"Until recently, yes. Served in Afghanistan for most of those years."

Shakir saw the confusion and hurt in her eyes begin to lift. He was glad he wasn't the cause of her pain anymore. But he wasn't sure where they went from here.

"Do you still love me?" she demanded suddenly.

"I… Yes, Nik. More than life itself. That's why I came today. I couldn't live without seeing you at least once again."

Flinging her arms around his neck, she pasted herself to his chest. "Then marry me! Be William's father and my husband. Stay with us. Love us and let's be a family."

With her bottom stretched halfway across his lap, his thigh hurt like a son of a bitch. But he almost didn't notice.

Here was everything he had always wanted and never thought he would have. Here was peace and love and someone who knew exactly what he was—and didn't care.

He kissed her hair and whispered his reply. She sighed deeply and kept on holding him tight. Her happiness rippled through him long afterward as he silently vowed to make her just this happy for the rest of their lives.

And sometime later, it occurred to him that the pleased sighs of the woman he loved were the most wonderful sounds he had ever heard in his entire life.

Epilogue

It was a quiet family ceremony on the beach with a soft breeze blowing in over the sun-kissed ocean waves. The bride and groom were barefoot in the sand. Not in the royal tradition at all, but the way Nikki had always dreamed it could be on the day of her wedding.

Well, it had been *quiet* for a while at first, she mused. Until three little boys became slightly bored and started to squirm. Chuckling to herself, she waved the children away to play in the sand and kissed her new husband. And kissed him again.

She would never tire of kissing Shakir. He looked handsome enough to eat today in his black tuxedo and stark white Bedouin head scarf. He made her feel like a princess.

It was a glorious spring day in the Mediterranean, with picturesque yachts anchored in the harbor. The ships' flags were unfurled and jewel-colored flowers adorned their sleek white decks. The many boats bobbing on crystal blue waters added to the romantic atmosphere.

Shakir's family surrounded them, congratulating and kissing her and patting him on the back. Everyone had something to say and well-wishes to add.

When most of the people wandered off down the beach to help themselves to champagne and cake, Tarik lingered behind. "I was just given a little bad news, brother."

"I don't want to hear it." Shakir pulled Nikki close and grinned. "It's too nice of a day."

She wrapped her arm as far around his waist as it would go and said, "Go ahead and say whatever you must, Tarik. All our days will be good ones from now on. And we know life goes on."

"A nice life sounds wonderful," Tarik told her with a sober nod. "But nothing will be really nice until we can convince the world authorities that the Taj Zabbar are terrorists."

He offered Shakir a congratulatory cigar and went on. "I've heard from my old bosses at D.O.D. They're not ready to admit publically that the facility at Kuh was a nuclear centrifuge in the making."

Shakir raised his shoulders. "No? What do we have to do to prove it, take them on a tour?"

"No, but it might've been helpful had we gotten a few pictures before we blew it up."

"Right. Sorry I forgot to bring along my camera." Shakir chewed on the end of the unlit cigar.

That brought a weak smile to Tarik's lips. Nikki was

glad. She wasn't used to seeing Tarik without his happy-go-lucky grin.

"I think we might have another chance to get our proof," Tarik told them. "Rumors are running rampant throughout the Taj organization about a big deal going down in a few weeks. Supposedly, one of the other elders has a line on buying the same kind of nuclear technology that they lost in Kuh. My guess is if they can't make the stuff themselves, then they think obtaining the same thing premade will be as good."

"Is that possible?" Shakir's eyes had grown dark. "I didn't think any of the countries in the world that'd developed nuclear weapons were in the position to sell them."

"Everything has a price, brother. And the Taj Zabbar are now wealthy enough to afford whatever the cost."

"This time we need proof." Shakir ground the cigar between his teeth.

"I'm working on a plan. By the time you return from your honeymoon, I'll have everything set up."

Tarik walked away as Shakir turned and pitched the cigar into the sea without ever lighting it.

The two lovers stood arm in arm, watching the children play near the ocean as the setting sun shot Valentine colors across the sky. A deep rosy glow brightened the land and sea.

"Are you sure you feel right about going away and leaving the boys in Darin and Rylie's care?" Shakir kept his voice soft and his arm around his new bride.

"I'm never felt surer of anything in my whole life. We have the rest of time for the children. I know you want to catch up for the years you lost with William, but you can't rush it. And the two of us come first."

Shakir tightened his grip on her waist, his woman, his love. "You're really something, you know that? Too smart for the likes of me."

She was his light and his life. "That idea you had for starting a 'lost children's' network in the Kadir name just about knocked me over it was so bloody brilliant. Our family's respectability and integrity will increase around the world exactly at the time when we need it the most. And," he added as he kissed the top of her head, "you will be the perfect person to head such an agency."

Nikki leaned against him and drew in a breath. She was perfect in every way. She was behind him in everything he did, and she gave him the family he'd always wanted but was afraid to dream about.

Tears backed up in his eyes as he thought of how close they'd come to never actually grasping this perfect love they'd found.

"Come show me how much you love me." She coyly shifted in his arms.

"I'll show you, all right," he promised. "Over and over for the bulk of the next four days on our holiday. And then again for every day afterward if I have my way."

He leaned down and kissed her, his embrace welcoming her to the home they would be making in each other's arms for the rest of their lives.

She was his love. His family. His forever.

* * * * *

COMING NEXT MONTH

Available January 25, 2011

#1643 NO ORDINARY HERO
Conard County: The Next Generation
Rachel Lee

#1644 IN HIS PROTECTIVE CUSTODY
The Doctors Pulaski
Marie Ferrarella

#1645 DEADLY VALENTINE
"Her Un-Valentine" by Justine Davis
"The February 14th Secret" by Cindy Dees

#1646 THE PRODIGAL BRIDE
The Bancroft Brides
Beth Cornelison

SRSCNM0111

REQUEST YOUR FREE BOOKS!

2 FREE NOVELS
PLUS
2 FREE GIFTS!

Silhouette®

ROMANTIC
SUSPENSE

Sparked by Danger, Fueled by Passion.

YES! Please send me 2 FREE Silhouette® Romantic Suspense novels and my 2 FREE gifts (gifts are worth about $10). After receiving them, if I don't wish to receive any more books, I can return the shipping statement marked "cancel." If I don't cancel, I will receive 4 brand-new novels every month and be billed just $4.24 per book in the U.S. or $4.99 per book in Canada. That's a saving of 15% off the cover price! It's quite a bargain! Shipping and handling is just 50¢ per book.* I understand that accepting the 2 free books and gifts places me under no obligation to buy anything. I can always return a shipment and cancel at any time. Even if I never buy another book from Silhouette, the two free books and gifts are mine to keep forever.

240/340 SDN E5Q4

Name	(PLEASE PRINT)	

Address		Apt. #

City	State/Prov.	Zip/Postal Code

Signature (if under 18, a parent or guardian must sign)

Mail to the **Silhouette Reader Service:**

IN U.S.A.: P.O. Box 1867, Buffalo, NY 14240-1867
IN CANADA: P.O. Box 609, Fort Erie, Ontario L2A 5X3

Not valid for current subscribers to Silhouette Romantic Suspense books.

Want to try two free books from another line?
Call 1-800-873-8635 or visit www.morefreebooks.com.

* Terms and prices subject to change without notice. Prices do not include applicable taxes. N.Y. residents add applicable sales tax. Canadian residents will be charged applicable provincial taxes and GST. Offer not valid in Quebec. This offer is limited to one order per household. All orders subject to approval. Credit or debit balances in a customer's account(s) may be offset by any other outstanding balance owed by or to the customer. Please allow 4 to 6 weeks for delivery. Offer available while quantities last.

Your Privacy: Silhouette is committed to protecting your privacy. Our Privacy Policy is available online at www.eHarlequin.com or upon request from the Reader Service. From time to time we make our lists of customers available to reputable third parties who may have a product or service of interest to you. If you would prefer we not share your name and address, please check here. ☐

Help us get it right—We strive for accurate, respectful and relevant communications. To clarify or modify your communication preferences, visit us at www.ReaderService.com/consumerschoice.

SRS10R

*Harlequin Romance author Donna Alward is loved
for her gorgeous rancher heroes.*

*Meet Wyatt as he's confronted by both a precious
little pink bundle left on his doorstep and his neighbor Elli
who's going to show him the ropes....*

Introducing
PROUD RANCHER, PRECIOUS BUNDLE

THE SQUAWKING QUIETED as Elli picked the baby up, and
Wyatt turned around, trying hard to ignore the feelings of
inadequacy as Darcy immediately stopped fussing.

"Maybe she's uncomfortable. What do you think, sweetheart?" Elli turned her conversation to the baby.

"What do you think is wrong?" Wyatt asked, putting the
coffee pot back on the burner.

A strange look passed over Elli's face, one that looked
like guilt and panic. But it was gone quickly. "I couldn't
say," she replied.

"But you were so good with her this afternoon." Wyatt
put his hands on his hips.

"Lucky, that's all. I just...remembered a few things."
The same strange look flitted over her features once more.

Wyatt took the coffee to the table. "You fooled me. You
looked like you knew exactly what you were doing." So
much so that Wyatt had felt completely inept. A feeling he
despised. He was used to being the one in control.

Elli and Darcy walked the length of the kitchen and
back. After a few moments, she admitted, "I haven't really
cared for a baby before. The things I thought of were simply
things I'd heard about. Not from experience, Mr. Black."

Her chin jutted up, closing the subject but making him

want to ask the questions now pulsing through his mind. But then he remembered the old saying—*Don't look a gift horse in the mouth.* He'd benefit from whatever insight she had and be glad of it.

"I don't really know what babies need," he said. "I fed her, patted her back like you did, walked her to sleep, but every time I put her down…"

Wyatt almost groaned. Of course. He'd forgotten one important thing. He'd been so focused on getting the formula the right temperature that he'd forgotten to check her diaper. Not that he had any clue what to do there either.

Pulling calves and shoveling out stalls was far less intimidating than one tiny newborn.

"She's probably due for a diaper change, isn't she." He tried to sound nonchalant. This was a perfect opportunity. Elli must know how to change a diaper. He could simply watch her so he'd know better for the next time.

Instead, Elli came around the corner of the counter and placed Darcy back in his arms. "Here you go, Uncle Wyatt," she said lightly. "You get diaper duty. I'll fix the coffee. Cream and sugar?"

Oh boy, Wyatt thought, looking down into Darcy's pursed face, his smug plan blown to smithereens. He was in for it now.

Will sparks fly between Elli and Wyatt?

Find out in
PROUD RANCHER, PRECIOUS BUNDLE
Available February 2011 from Harlequin Romance

Try these Healthy and Delicious Spring Rolls!

INGREDIENTS

2 packages rice-paper
spring roll wrappers
(20 wrappers)

1 cup grated carrot

¼ cup bean sprouts

1 cucumber, julienned

1 red bell pepper, without
stem and seeds, julienned

4 green onions
finely chopped—
use only the green part

DIRECTIONS

1. Soak one rice-paper wrapper
   in a large bowl of hot water
   until softened.

2. Place a pinch each of carrots,
   sprouts, cucumber, bell
   pepper and green onion on the
   wrapper toward the bottom
   third of the rice paper.

3. Fold ends in and roll tightly
   to enclose filling.

4. Repeat with remaining
   wrappers. Chill before
   serving.

Silhouette Desire

USA TODAY bestselling author

ELIZABETH BEVARLY

is back with a steamy and powerful story.

Gavin Mason is furious and vows revenge on high-price, high-society girl Violet Tandy. Her novel is said to be fiction, but everyone *knows* she's referring to Gavin as a client in her memoir. The tension builds when they learn not to judge a book by its cover.

THE BILLIONAIRE GETS HIS WAY

Available February wherever books are sold.

Always Powerful, Passionate and Provocative.